CONTRARY PEOPLE

Other books by Carolyn Osborn:

A Horse of Another Color

The Fields of Memory

The Grands

Warriors & Maidens

Uncertain Ground

CONTRARY PEOPLE

A Novel

CAROLYN OSBORN

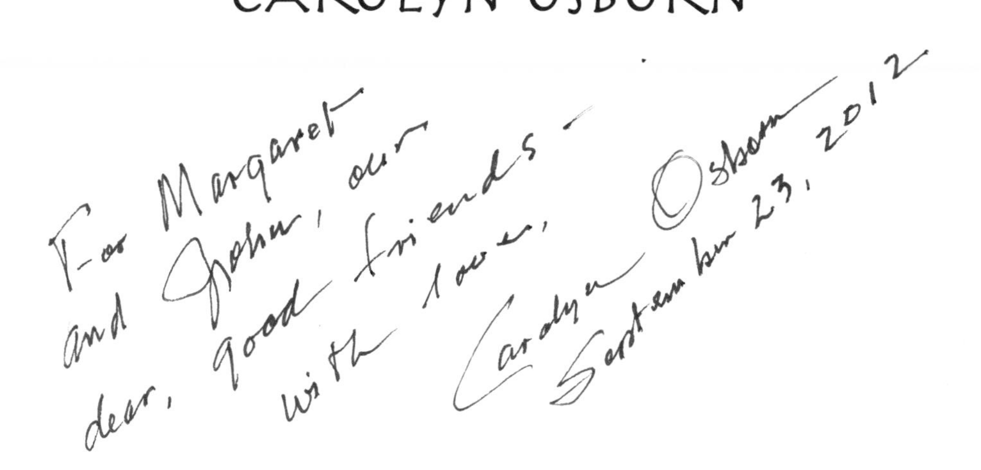

WingsPress

San Antonio, Texas
2012

Stories excerpted from this novel first appeared
in *The Texas Quarterly* and *The Antioch Review*.

First Edition
Print Edition ISBN: 978-0-916727-96-3
ePub ISBN: 978-1-60940-216-7
Kindle ISBN: 978-1-60940-217-4
PDF ISBN: 978-1-60940-218-1

Wings Press
627 E. Guenther
San Antonio, Texas 78210
Phone/fax: (210) 271-7805

On-line catalogue and ordering:
www.wingspress.com
All Wings Press titles are distributed to the trade by
Independent Publishers Group
www.ipgbook.com

Library of Congress Cataloging-in-Publication Data:

Osborn, Carolyn, 1934-
Contrary people : a novel / Carolyn Osborn. -- 1st ed.
p. cm.
ISBN 978-0-916727-96-3 (pbk., printed edition : alk. paper)
-- ISBN 978-1-60940-216-7 (epub ebook) -- ISBN 978-1-60940-217-4 (kindle ebook) -- ISBN 978-1-60940-218-1 (library pdf ebook)
1. Older people--Fiction. 2. Austin (Tex.)--Fiction. 3. Texas--History--20th century--Fiction. I. Title.
PS3565.S348C66 2012
813'.54--dc23

2011048301

For Joe Osborn

CONTRARY PEOPLE

1967

Note to the reader: The terminology of the times is reflected in *Contrary People.* "Mexican" was used at the time to indicate both Mexicans and Mexican-Americans.

CHAPTER ONE

It was usually quiet at the museum on Saturdays when Theo Isaac was there. An obscure place in Austin, a small city where there were few obscurities, it was seldom visited. Those who had lived there for a long time like Theo, the exceptionally curious tourist, lonely women with an unexpected hour on their hands, mothers who thought their children ought to learn to appreciate sculpture—these were the usual visitors to the Elisabet Ney Museum. In the midst of a block of park land, well back from the streets, surrounded by straggling cedar trees and high bushes, protected in front by a low rock wall, it welcomed the general public with an open gate and a path leading to the front door, but the general public, Theo had observed, did not often come to see what Miss Ney had left them.

Saturday was his day to serve as the museum's keeper. All week long he looked forward to the one day he would be impeccably dressed in his only black suit with his gold watch chain stretched opulently across his vest instead of crumpled in his side pocket. Other days he went around in his shirtsleeves and whatever trousers he could find that didn't need mending. He was down to two pair of presentable trousers, not including the pair matching his suit, but he wasn't going to buy any new clothes. He could have afforded to if he wanted to, he assured himself; however, it would be a waste. If he was careful they could bury him in his black suit, and he was careful. Every speck of lint was brushed off before and after each wearing, and he had the suit cleaned when necessary.

He walked to the museum every Saturday morning, a small neat man doing his civic duty in his funeral clothes. He thought of his part-time job as a favor he could do the city where he had lived most of his seventy years although he took the dollar-per-hour pay they gave him. He was still worth a dollar an hour! As he had enough to keep him, pay any hospital bills, and bury him decently with something left over for his two sons, he donated his salary to the upkeep of the museum. It was not, he felt, an outright bribe. He put the bills in the iron box in the front hall with the sign *Voluntary Contributions* posted above it; if he wanted he could always donate the thirty-five dollars a month to some other institution. The city needed someone at the Elisabet Ney on Saturdays, and he needed something to do.

He settled himself at the small desk behind a glass case filled with plaques of women's faces and a cast of the head of an infant made after the child's death, an example, in his opinion, of morbid Victorian sentimentality and unfortunate taste. However the need to memorialize a child was an emotion Ney obviously understood, and when he considered it more closely, the necessity was even greater then when so many more children were lost early.

Directly behind him double wooden doors were shut against March drafts; above the doors the only daylight in the room filtered through a wide north window rapidly being overgrown by a jungle of pot plants on the sill. In one corner the stone fireplace had been boarded up to enclose an electric heater now buzzing and glowing in an effort to take the chill out of the stone walls. Though the ceiling was high, and the stones must have been cold early in the morning, the place was much too warm. He felt like a wizened plant in a dry greenhouse.

To his immediate right was a cast of the bust of William Jennings Bryan; to his left was Dr. Prather, one of the ex-presidents of the University of Texas, where Theo had taught history. Dr. Prather, viewers were informed by the little piece of cardboard leaning against his chest, had been the first man known to give voice to the immortal phrase "the eyes of Texas are upon you." Theo doubted President Prather had known he was immortalizing himself with a phrase, but that was only one more of the kinks of fate that allowed a man to be remembered by one thing he'd said rather than by anything he'd done. Prather was also known as one of Robert E. Lee's students,

Theo remembered, laughing silently at himself for having the historian's habit of storing odd details to pepper his lectures so his students might have ways to memorize dates. Straight across the room in his line of vision from his seat at the desk was a bust of one of the governors of Texas, a rather grim looking old man. He preferred to shift his eyes to the pleasant ringleted head of another governor's daughter. All the Europeans except Miss Ney, who had been German, and her husband, a Scot, were segregated in an adjoining room. Theo was encircled by Texas governors, judges, heroes, and oil portraits of Miss Ney and her patrons. He surveyed the room, acknowledging as he usually did, that if his part-time job did not provide much human companionship, it did give him the company of some distinguished ghosts. Pale casts of real people. Oh, dear God! Had he become the same? He pressed a thin blue vein on the back of his hand. Faint life there pumping away.

He led, he reflected, a part-time life. He was a part-time sleeper, a part-time cook, a part-time dog-walker, a continual mourner. His wife had been dead for two years, and his recurrent wishful dream was she was still alive. Yet she'd died a miserable death. Cancer ate her up. When she was gone everyone said it was a merciful death. He agreed at the time, knowing it was better for her anguish to die, but he would have given the days he had left to him to hear her voice calling his name, to hear her plaintive voice calling him to come to her room and turn her over.

"Who is the man handcuffed to the rock?"

Startled out of his daydream by the intensity of the question, he twisted around in his chair to look at a boy.

"How did you get in?" He was a small Mexican boy with a jagged haircut and old but well-shined shoes. His clothes were clean and neatly pressed. Evidently his mother cared how he looked. A smudge of dust on his forehead showed he didn't pay much attention to himself. He must have been running his hands over the sculptures. Some of them were not very well dusted.

"The back door." The boy pointed to the room where the Europeans were collected. "It was open." He walked around to the side and braced himself with one dirty hand against the facing glass case. Yes, he must have been touching the statues. Good sculpture should arouse the tactile sense, though he did not think Miss Ney's figures often did. Who wanted to pat an old baron's stony head—not the children dragged in by culture-conscious mothers. The only thing that ever interested them was Stephen F. Austin's plaster gun and the fact it didn't shoot was always a disappointment to the little machine-age monsters.

"Yes, I remember. I unlocked the door this morning." Theo tapped the glass top with his dry fingers. The child had asked him something. What was it? He should answer. Visitors hardly ever asked him anything. When he'd first started working he'd followed people around from room to room commenting on Miss Ney and her work, chattering he soon perceived, mostly to himself. He retired to his desk to sit as mute as the rest of the statues. After all those years standing in front of classes, the lack of attention made him feel unappreciated at first, but he understood now that few people wanted great blocs of information. Musing attention was most viewers' general response. Gradually he'd come to accept it simply as any museumgoer's glazed vision. He had the same reaction himself when he went to other museums if he stayed over an hour. The child had asked about a statue, the man handcuffed to the rock.

"It isn't a statue exactly. It's a cast, a plaster cast taken from a statue of Prometheus, the god who brought fire to men." It was the only nude in the museum; that's what probably interested the boy more than anything else.

"Why is he handcuffed to the rock?"

"He is being punished. Those old Greek gods knew how to punish. Because he gave the fire away, Zeus had him chained to a high mountain and—" The child was too young to know anything about mythology. He could not tell him about the vulture descending each day.

"Does it hurt him?" The boy looked at his own skinny arms.

"Please tell me your name."

"Is he real? Does it hurt him?" He stretched his arms out by his sides.

"Yes, it hurts. He does not complain though."

"I am called Ricardo. I am eight. Where is the mountain at?"

Theo sucked in his lower lip in an effort not to correct him then let it go. "Between the a and the t," he snapped, the pedagogue in him overcoming caution. He sighed, another one demanding to be taught. He used to see children like that in his classes. They couldn't be stopped and neither could this one. Why, after all, should he be? It was a brutal story, no more brutal than many fairy tales though, nor half as vivid as a television murder, or the daily pictures of men fighting and dying in Vietnam.

"If you are eight, Ricardo, you are old enough to read. Go to the library and ask for a book about Prometheus. Here. This will tell you all about the museum." He lifted a folder from the top of a large pile and slid it across the case toward the boy.

Ricardo's hand closed over the paper; he crunched it into a ball and stuck it in his pocket. "Where is the library?"

Theo opened the desk drawer and pulled out a city map. "You are here at the museum. Do you see?"

Ricardo nodded.

"Here is the library down here near the city hall. How can you get down there from here?"

"I can go anywheres on my bicycle."

"Good. Go to the library then come back and tell me about Prometheus."

"You already know." The boy left Theo's side and ran out the front door. The museum keeper waited a moment then got up and followed him. Ricardo was riding away on a bicycle much too large for him. He had to throw most of his weight from one side to another in order to reach the pedals. The child was determined, but he seemed so wary. Of course, he could have told him about Prometheus, still if he'd told him Ricardo would have forgotten. Probably he was more curious about his fig leaf than the myth. Perhaps he wasn't even on his way to the library. Children were often intensely interested in something they forgot in five minutes. It was better, sometimes, to be stingy with knowledge. They used to argue about that, he and Kate. Give, she'd say, give all you've got. No, you must withhold something unless you want parrots uttering your own thoughts. It's a long way to the library, miles, and that child has to struggle with his enormous bicycle. I know it, Kate! Don't exaggerate!

"Tim!" he called turning away from the door. There was no answer. Where was he? Cleaning and dusting somewhere. He'd been maintaining the museum years before Theo had started to work.

"Tim?" His voice wavered, a thin echo preceding him through the hall.

"Up here," Tim's answer rolled down. He seemed to be somewhere outside, but there were no repairs needed on the tiny front balcony, which with a storeroom comprised the second level. Plenty of dusting should be done in the big sculpture-filled rooms downstairs by the look of Ricardo's hands.

He started up the narrow wooden steps. "What are you doing?" They were always shouting, he and Tim, like two small boys delighting in the noise they could make in the vacant rooms.

Tim roared again. "Washing windows. I'm sitting here on this window sill, and I'm about to fall off."

Theo sighed. Terrible things were always about to happen to Tim and they never did. "Which room are you in?" He stood at the top of the stairs. A winding circular fire escape led to a tower room on the third level. He hoped Tim wasn't up there. He didn't like to make the stiff climb, and the anatomical studies stacked on shelves, hands without arms, feet without legs, mortally depressed him.

"I'm in the storeroom, part way in anyways."

Theo entered the storeroom. Tim's body filled the window in one corner. As the frames were mounted on hinges allowing both halves to be swung inside like French doors, it was completely unnecessary for anyone to perch on the sill while washing them. He eyed Tim narrowly, wondering if the simple idea of imminent danger made life more exciting for him. Then he glanced around the room. The entire place had been emptied and cleaned, the walls covered with white burlap, and all the woodwork painted white. Tim's skin appeared even blacker in the middle of so much white.

"What's going on up here?"

Tim stood up, being careful not to catch his starched white jacket on the sill. He wore the jacket for every job. Theo didn't know who had provided it, some former employer probably. It made him look more like a butler than a janitor, perhaps his reason for wearing it all the time. Tim lived in jovial yet firm opposition to certain social and legal rules, and he was his own authority on what constituted dignity.

"Don't you know? We're having a art gallery in here. I been cleaning all week."

"An art gallery? But we have that downstairs."

"Yes, but this one's going to be pictures."

"What kind of pictures? Whose pictures?" Theo gazed at the blank white walls trying to imagine pictures hung on them.

"Modren, they say. Modren artists are going to send some."

He sucked in his lip and closed his eyes in pain. It wasn't Tim's language he minded; he'd grown accustomed to that. Since he'd determined from the first never to play the officious boss, he'd never attempted to correct him. What outraged him was the idea of contemporary paintings at the Ney Museum. They would clash terribly with the nineteenth-century sculpture making Miss Ney's work appear more outdated than ever. He shuddered at visions of bright gashes of color across the walls.

"It seems funny to me," said Tim, "but I guess it will draw more people in."

Theo opened his eyes and looked at Tim's comforting face. All his life one black person or another—a maid, a yardman, a janitor—had been telling him things were going to be all right. They knew and he knew things were not going to be anywhere near right . . . still he appreciated the soothing voices. "I grow old . . . I grow old," he murmured to himself. "I am hardly even growing old anymore—I am old."

"Well," Tim shrugged, "so am I."

"How old are you?"

"Sixty-five, but you don't tell it, please. If the Social Security finds out I got this job still, they'll cut me off."

He was confused about Social Security rules, Theo thought, but Tim wouldn't appreciate being told. And, he was also sure, he was equally uncertain about those rules himself.

"I haven't got anybody to tell and I wouldn't anyway. A man ought to be able to work as long as he wants to work."

"I don't so much want to as I have to. You know."

Theo nodded. "I know." Tim's wife had to stay at home to care for two grandchildren whose father had disappeared. Their mother, Tim's daughter, worked as a maid six days a week. Their combined salaries took care of five people. He didn't know how. It had been difficult for him at times to support a wife and only two sons on a teacher's pay.

He waved his arm in front of him to indicate the room. "This must have taken you all week."

"Yes. A whole lot of old junk had to be moved to the cellar. I nearly broke my hip on them stairs."

"Did you do the painting too?" Theo moved closer. "Yes, you did. You've got paint on your glasses. How can you see with them all spattered like that?"

"Used to the spots now." Tim grinned. "The whole world's gone polka-dotted."

Theo surveyed the room again. "It looks good."

Tim touched the wall with his outspread hand. "Yes, it looks so good I hate to think of anybody nailing a nail in it, and I'm probably the very one that'll have to do it." His hand slid off the wall. "Nobody told you?"

Theo shook his head. "No reason for anybody on the board to call me and tell me what they're doing. I just work here." He began walking about the room peering out the windows. The original glass, bubbled and wavy, was still in some of them. Through these panes the flowering quince looked like soft pink streaks and the surrounding park a haze of colors, but the new glass showed the trees should have been trimmed in January, and the grass was patched with brown. By the end of summer the lawn would be brown all over. Decay was not pleasant to watch even though he felt at home in the middle of it. Most of all it offended his years of gardening experience. A well-tended one could be a delight. Some days he longed to begin weeding and pruning, but the whole park was beyond his strength. His own yard wasn't. Kate wouldn't be there though, wouldn't be forking soil, weeding, fussing at him for cutting the spirea and photenia back too far.

"We ought to water more."

"Yes, I ought to," agreed Tim. "All week I been up here though. Seems like when I have to work on the inside the outside has to slide, and when I work outside the inside—"

"I thought the city sent men to work on the grounds."

"They sends them now and then. All they got time to do is mow and trim a little. Maybe with this exhibition going on they will send some more. I have about got a permanent bend in the middle from toting them hoses around."

"When are the pictures supposed to arrive?"

"Anytime from today on. The show's not going to be for a month. They need a lot of notice I guess."

"Yes . . . well." Theo pulled out a gold pocket watch that had been his father's. "It's eleven-thirty. I'm going back down and get my lunch."

He walked slowly down the stairs. Harder on the heart going down, they said, than going up. There were few restaurants near the museum, so he brought some sandwiches and a vacuum bottle filled with tea to work with him in a brown paper sack he saved from his weekly visit to the grocery store. Kate had gone to the store every day. She was forever running out of something or deciding, at the last minute, to try a new recipe. He went only once a week. The other old people there bothered him, the widows who continued to go every day to buy one frozen pot pie and to begin a conversation with anyone who'd listen. It was cowardly to go to the grocery every day out of sheer loneliness. When he did go, Mrs. Dickens, the widow of a college professor, she never ceased reminding him, was always pecking around the green vegetables, an old hen in search of another rooster.

He leaned over the glass case to get his lunch out of the desk drawer, pushing the pile of folders into a sprawling heap. "Lord God in heaven most high!" He drew out the curse turning it into a supplication before he was finished. At least once every Saturday he knocked over the folders. Stacking them up again, he wondered what it would have been like to have been married to Elisabet Ney. The picture of her on front of each folder, taken from a painting done in 1859, showed her standing by the bust she'd made of King George V, the last king of Hanover. Part of the king's profile was shown, a brooding, mustachioed shadow. Elisabet's left arm rested against the stand holding the figure. She had a long face, a long straight nose, dark eyes, dark curly hair, and a determined expression. In her right hand, against the soft folds of her long dress, she held a curved clay-modeling tool. Born in Germany in 1833, the daughter of a master stonecutter, she became a sculptor. Somehow she made the Art Academy in Munich accept her as a student, a young woman demanding to be taught an art open to very few women. While she lived in Europe she made busts and statues of famous people: Jacob Grimm, Schopenhauer, Garibaldi, Ludwig II, the mad king of Bavaria. She ended in Texas making statues of state heroes, governors, and friends.

A formidable woman, she cut her hair short, wore trousers to mount her scaffolds, kept her maiden name, and called her husband "my best friend." Ney was one of those nineteenth-century heroines who hammered and chipped until the strictures of convention left her free to hammer and chip. The museum had been her studio and her home. From the outside it resembled a small stone fortress built onto a Greek temple.

Her best friend, Dr. Montgomery, stayed over a hundred miles away at their farm, Liendo plantation, making various scientific experiments and writing philosophical treatises. They had two sons, one who died young and another who grew up at the plantation. For a while, when the children were little, Miss Ney stayed at home with them, but after the first child died and the second grew older, she built her temple fortress. There was a lot of conjecture about whether she and Dr. Montgomery were really married. They were—it had been proven by some busybody who looked up the certificate—but compared to the quiet life he and Kate had lived together, Elisabet Ney and Edmund Montgomery were a dashing pair. Theo put down the collected folders with a thump. Had he ever done anything dashing?

He'd broken off a branch of his mother's prize flowering peach tree when he was fifteen and carried it like a banner before him to give to a girl. The blossoms had fallen off by the time he was halfway to her house. He had volunteered for World War I, more out of a desire to see France than from patriotic motives, and all he saw was the inside of a hospital. He caught influenza two days after his ship docked at Le Havre. He had followed the regular course of a man's life: married, fathered sons, had a profession, retired, lost his wife. His life had been filled with commonplaces, the usual virtues, the general sins, and there was very little time left for anything unusual to happen to him. Perhaps he should develop some amazing eccentricity? He could wear his coat backward, throw his garbage over the backyard neighbors' fence, call May Dickens an old bitch to her face. Ah, no. Wearing his coat backward would be uncomfortable, he liked his neighbors, and May Dickens was only a lonely old widow. He could dye his white hair blue. That wouldn't hurt anyone. Cake coloring would probably do the job. He would be forgiven for his blue hair because of his age. Here comes Mr. Isaac, he's harmless really, an old man with a passion for blue. It would be a nuisance. He'd never wanted to be stared at. Why, at seventy, was he thinking of reverting to adolescence? The mind played tricks. Was his failing? Preposterous! His body would fail him before his mind was gone. The last hope of the elderly.

"Remember," he grinned at himself in the washroom mirror, "to hire someone to hit you over the head the minute senility sets in." The door wobbled to and fro behind him as he walked out. Naturally, he couldn't think of a person he could pay to do such a thing. In this paradox, he found a certain ludicrous comfort.

The balcony, with its dark red painted floorboards and two enormous green metal stars between the railings, was his favorite part of the museum. Under a live oak tree in the back Tim was eating his lunch. When he got through he would remove his white jacket and lie down in the sun for a nap. Theo would have joined him, but he did not want to take off his own jacket to sprawl on the grass; he might get grass stains on his vest and trousers. He preferred his rooftop view where he could watch the birds rummaging in the branches and smell the strong purple flowers of the mountain laurel tree below, a funeral smell. A funeral tree? No, it was too weak to hold dead weight. He approved of the Comanche burial; they flung their dead in trees to be picked clean by buzzards . . . better than rotting underground, but who could stand the odor of corruption or the bloody sight of the feast? He shuddered at his morbidity. Forty years of teaching American history, forty years of trying to follow its pattern. Disorderly as it was, he wanted to believe in some progress and, as usual, discovered himself in the midst of the wilderness of his own mind.

A car stopped in front of the gate; a young woman in white slacks and a loud yellow shirt bolted out of it. She opened the back door, pulled out a canvas, and came hurrying across the lawn with it in both hands.

"Hello," she called. "Are you open?"

"Closed for lunch." Theo poured himself some tea and took a sip.

"Can I leave this here? It's a picture for your opening."

He bit into his sandwich—ham. He'd made it himself at seven that morning, and five hours later he'd already forgotten what he'd packed for lunch. He couldn't understand why he brought ham sandwiches. They made him so thirsty. He looked over the railing again. The girl was still waiting.

"The door isn't locked. You can leave it in the hall," he said, annoyed at himself for his forgetfulness and the girl for her persistence.

"I'd like to see where it's going to be hung."

"The gallery's up here."

"I'll bring it up then," the girl shouted cheerfully.

Before he could answer he heard her running up the stairs. He threw the rest of the sandwich back into his sack and drank his tea. The girl popped out on his balcony.

"Beautiful! I'm sorry I've never been out here before. I'm Melrose Davis." She sat down on the railing facing him.

Theo glared at her. Her hair was almost as yellow as her shirt, dyed probably, and her slacks were too tight across her bottom.

"I know who you are, Mr. Isaac. My grandmother told me you might be here. I'm Rose Davis's granddaughter."

"Rose Davis's—?"

The girl bobbed her head. A long hank of hair, fastened by a rubber band on the back of her head, flapped when she moved.

"She's the only one of my grandmothers still living. The other one was named Melinda. My parents glued Melinda and Rose together and got Melrose. Isn't it tacky!"

Theo blinked. Rose Davis, when she was a girl, had complained of her name, not in the least original she'd said, and she deserved an original name. He didn't know she was back. She'd been gone for so many years.

"How is your grandmother?"

"Rosie's fine. She and I are the only ones in the family who get along. Everyone else is still semi-shocked." Melrose made a face. "The truth is they were more comfortable when she was in Paris."

"Yes, I suppose so." He smiled.

Rose Davis went to Europe on a tour in 1950 and simply did not come home. Though she was forty-five at the time, half the town was sure she had a lover. The mere notion of lovers in Paris was a crowd pleaser. Her friends could say little to defend her as Rose never bothered to explain her actions to anyone. She had enough money of her own to do as she pleased and, within a year, she had a divorce—another source of extensive eyebrow raising.

At that time it was customary for gentlemen to allow their wives to divorce them quietly and without contest. Any opprobrium resulting was silently carried on manly shoulders. Rose, however, reversed the convention by letting Edward Davis divorce her. Possibly she did not want to return to the state in order to initiate the procedure; more likely though, knowing Rose, she may have thought Edward had every right to divorce her. Whatever disgrace resulted did not reach her across the Atlantic. Why had she returned? Was she back to stay? How did she know he worked at the museum? Perhaps someone told her. Had he seen her somewhere and failed to recognize her?

All these questions flitted through his mind as he showed Melrose through the museum. She didn't like the anatomical studies any more than he did. Tim had moved some of them to a case in the hallway. Silly bits and pieces, she said. Why should a museum—even one devoted to one artist—keep every single thing, or why, since they had, did it all have to be displayed at one time?

Arriving in the new gallery where she'd leaned her picture against the wall, he took one furtive downward look and recoiled. It was a picture of a flat tire, realistic, enormous and terribly flat, lying on a highway going from nowhere to nowhere. A useless, purposeless object, it made him feel older and more worn-out than he actually was.

"Why this?" he said, making his voice as colorless as he could.

"I don't know—*épater les bourgeois*, I guess. I wanted to see if I could do that sort of thing."

Theo could feel the steam of indignation rising inside his head. He had to let a little of it out. "It's rather depressing."

"Do you think so? Rosie thought it was funny, but she's been in France so long she thinks most everything going on here is funny." Melrose gave the room a quick professional glance. "The light's fine now, but you're going to have to get some supplementary spots for the late afternoon."

"This was Miss Ney's bedroom. It was never intended for a picture gallery. She built the light she needed for her work into the house. You'll see nothing but north windows in the studio rooms downstairs." He continued on down in silence half listening to Melrose chatter about the importance of indirect lighting, the best-lit museums she'd seen. They went into the first studio room.

"They're all plaster!"

"Yes, most of them are. After all, she was working on commission. You can't expect people to give their marble statues back to the museum."

He left her to confront the Texans. The past, by sheer weight of history, would vindicate him. What was a flat tire on a lonely road? Nothing. Retiring to his desk he watched her circling the room. She paused for a moment in front of Dr. Montgomery and said something about his beard. Terribly talkative girl, like her grandmother. Kate had been a quiet woman. They had a lot to talk about though, married forty-three years and still had a lot to say to each other . . . both of them sitting in the living room remembering their sons, their students—she'd taught English at the local high school—their summer vacations in Mexico, the year in England when he had a research grant, their long mutual pasts, and in the end, during the last week of her life, all she said was his name, Theo. He dozed. Melrose tiptoed past him on her way out. Theo barely heard her; he'd begun dreaming of two empty rocking chairs on either side of a fireplace filled with ashes. He entered the room and pushed first one chair then the other, so they were rocking to and fro gently. When he quit pushing they both stopped absolutely still. The sight of the stilled chairs frightened him, and he ran from the room. He awoke knowing fresh grief, knowing he did not mourn his wife's death as much as he feared his own.

He looked over the visitors' book. Ricardo had not signed it, but Melrose had printed her name in fat letters. Didn't they teach them how to write anymore? She'd given her address too, a street in the older section of town near the university. He studied the street number for a moment then remembered why it was familiar; it must have been the house Rose Davis had lived in as a girl. She had come back to it, and her granddaughter was living there with her. Strange. Yet why shouldn't she come back to her home, and after so many years, how could anything Rose did seem peculiar? It would have been peculiar for her to do the expected, to remain in France and die there, forgotten except by a few old gossips who'd go to their reward soon enough. She stayed with Edward twenty-five years or longer, and just as everyone had ceased to wonder if they were going to remain together, shortly after their son had married, Rose vanished on her tour. She seemed possessed by the ability to do the unexpected at the proper time.

Who are they? Theo raised his head like an old hunting dog sniffing the wind. A couple holding hands entered the door letting their hands drop to their sides as they passed. He had seen the woman before but not the man. She lived in his neighborhood; he was certain he'd met her out walking with her children. She and the man could have been brother and sister; both of them were young and fair, the tops of their heads streaked lighter by the sun, and they had similar expressions on their faces—hunger. No, they were not kin, couldn't be, and the man was not her husband. He had seen the husband. So, she had a lover. That was it. They were lovers. He was delighted. He'd caught a glimpse of a marvelous secret; he was warmed by the air enveloping them. Oh! He was a disgusting old man, warming himself at someone else's fire, probably take up window peeking next. What was he to do with himself? Did Kate ever have a lover? No, she wasn't the sort of woman for that. What is the sort? She was not a sensual woman, but she might have been warmer for someone else. Who? Was he jealous of the dead? He'd never questioned her faithfulness while she was living. Perhaps some other man had made her happier than he did. He couldn't begrudge her that. He'd been faithful, forty-three years he'd been faithful, in body if not in mind. He'd looked at other women, and he'd had his share of lusty feelings, but he'd never done a thing . . . kissed people on New Year's politely on the cheek, never even patted a passing fanny. He had been a ninny, a namby-pamby, a respected member of the faculty.

There was Ricardo again. The smudge of dust was still on his forehead, and he'd ripped the edge of one pants leg at the bottom, caught it on his bicycle chain probably.

"What have you got?"

"A picture. See." He held it up to Theo's face.

Theo frowned. It was a picture of Christ showing his bleeding heart. A cross was glowing in the middle of the heart. "Why have you brought this?"

"His insides are showing . . . like Prometheus."

"Hmn." He murmured and placed the picture face down in front of him. Did the child love the bloody figure or was it only that "insides" fascinated him? "You went to the library?"

"Yes, on my bicycle. I find it."

"Found," Theo corrected automatically. "And you found the book?"

"A lady found it for me. She let me hold it, and I sat down there and read. They have chairs and tables."

"Yes. You could have taken the book home with you if you wanted."

"I know," the boy said scornfully. "At home my baby sister tears up books." He picked up the picture and put it in his shirt pocket. "The statue in there. It is not true."

"It is a myth," said Theo carefully.

"A vulture came every day and pecked his liver out, and it growed back every day. The statue isn't right. His liver isn't showing. Why didn't they show his liver? They didn't show it in the book either and they didn't tell me where the mountain is."

"Not they, she."

"She?"

"The lady who made the statue."

"A lady made that?"

Theo nodded. "She made everything in this museum."

"How could she?"

"With some talent and a lot of time."

"Could I do it?"

"Perhaps, if you had the proper training."

"If I made a statue of Prometheus, I would make it better than a woman. I would not be afraid to show his insides."

"That statue was important to Miss Ney, Ricardo. She always wanted to do Prometheus. Come, let me show you someone else she was interested in." He got up from the desk intending to take him into the next room and show him the figure of Ludwig II, but he could hear the voices of the young couple. They were quarreling. He delayed entering and began talking to Ricardo again. He was sure the young woman knew who he was. That was good, to be known when he was so old he hardly believed in his own shadow any longer. He had been recognized; he had to be avoided. Negative recognition was better than none at all. He wished he could tell her she need not avoid him; her secret was hers to keep.

"Look," he indicated a bas-relief of a young boy's head. "See how carefully this has been done. It's cut in hard stone, but see how soft the cheek and curls seem."

"How old is he?"

"I'm not sure. What do you think?"

Ricardo stared at the child's face. "Five maybe. He is a baby still."

Theo heard the voices in the next room diminish. They had found the back door. He led Ricardo past the statues of Austin and Houston to Ludwig.

"Here is a king who went mad."

"He has a lot of clothes on. Why is he so dressed up?"

Ludwig, arrayed in a richly patterned doublet and flowing cloak, stared over their heads, frozen in his flummery and fine nonchalance.

"He admired the king of France, Louis the fourteenth, and he tried to copy everything he'd done. Louis was extravagant in his dress, so Ludwig dressed up also." He looked at the boy who was gaping at him. "He loved costumes."

"Like Halloween?"

"Somewhat."

"Can I go up there?" Ricardo pointed to a raised platform built into the south corner. A hammock hung from the ceiling above it.

"Yes, but don't try the hammock. It's old, and the rope is rotten by now."

Ricardo ran up the stairs. "She sleep up here?"

"I doubt it. She probably slept in bed like everybody else. Somebody found that around the house and strung it up there."

"This high up I see everything."

"She could have a different view of her sculptures from there. It's important to be able to see from all angles." Theo walked over to the side of the cast of Prometheus and touched the plaster leg, stained and worn smooth where many others had touched it.

"This was not a commissioned piece . . . no one paid her to do it." He stumbled in his explanation not knowing how much the child could understand. "You are looking down on it, but I think she intended for people to look up to him. She cared about the gift of fire Prometheus gave to man. She never intended to show his insides."

"Do you know where the mountain is?" Ricardo started down the stairs. He had not touched the hammock.

"In the Caucasus, I believe." He thought of telling him the mountains were in Asia, but didn't. All the child wanted was a name; the mountain could be anywhere.

Ricardo stopped at the bottom of the steps and pointed to the open back door. "A man and a woman are out there." He snorted. "They are kissing."

Theo suppressed the beginning of a smile.

Leaning over the stair rail, Ricardo looked down at the figure to his right. "Albert Sidney Johnston 1803 to 1862. Poor Albert Sidney Johnston, only fifty-nine when he died. The card says he's in the state cemetery. He has a flag for a blanket. Why did they wrap him in a flag?"

"He was a Confederate general from Texas who was killed on the battleground of Shiloh. He died in a strange way. He was hit in the leg with a bullet and bled to death before he realized his wound was serious. That's a Confederate flag draped over him. Maybe you could get a book on the Civil War."

"Was Albert Sidney Johnston a hero like Prometheus?"

"Prometheus brought the gift of fire to man and endured the torture of the vulture without complaint until Hercules set him free. That is the myth. Judge for yourself."

"His liver growed back, didn't it?"

"It grew, yes. Every day it grew back, and he provided a new feast for the vulture."

"Albert Sidney Johnston was lucky. He didn't have no vulture."

"A vulture," said Theo.

In the late afternoon, close to five, Theo walked home slowly although his house wasn't far away. It had turned into a hotter day than he'd expected, and, as he grew older, he found the summers more wearing partially because they started so early in Texas. This year he might have to turn on the air-conditioning in April. The last thing he'd done before leaving was to help

Tim set up the sprinklers on the lawn. Tim did the hardest part; he got the hoses out of the cellar where they lay coiled like sleeping serpents. Then Theo helped him drag them over the ground and position the sprinklers so the brown patches would get a good soaking. It seemed like the first physical labor he'd done in years, which wasn't exactly true since he continued to water his own yard in a desultory way. However his weeding would never have satisfied Kate. It was a job he did mainly when he had the mulligrubs, the days when the war news, bad weather, or his own loneliness grew oppressive. Those were the times he turned his temper loose on the invading Bermuda grass, wild carrots, and chickweed. The same weeds appeared at the Ney along with a host of dandelions every spring. Since he and Tim hadn't been hired to do the city's gardening, the weeds got watered along with the grass. Tim, working alone, put the sprinklers anywhere. Hypnotized by the mere sound of water running, he'd be convinced the grass was being watered when all he was doing was spraying the same old places. They made a good team since Tim was more exacting than he was about interior repairs, especially those involving painting and plumbing. Years of marriage, years of mowing lawns, shaping bushes, and taming unruly vines, Theo supposed, gave him some expertise on how yards should be done.

A boy passing on a bicycle reminded him of Ricardo. It had been a peculiar day. First Ricardo, then Melrose, then the young couple, all of them totally unlike any of the usual museum visitors, all of them coming for purposes unknown, unguessed at by the museum's founder. Ricardo, playing in the park, wandered in by accident. Melrose came, not to see Ney's sculptures, but to submit some of her own work. The lovers sought privacy. His pace slowed to a shuffle. Worse than heat or fatigue was the remembrance he had no one at home to tell any of his day to—no one but Homer, the half-deaf dog Kate had left him. Sometimes he hated Homer for being there when Kate wasn't. Most of the time he was glad for the dog's company.

Dazed by a sudden hunger for conversation, he walked past the street where he usually turned to go home. When he reached the next corner he looked up to read the street sign, white letters on an orange background. How long had it been since he'd really seen one? They used to be a different color. Orange and white were the colors of the university. Chamber of Commerce loyalty must have changed the color of the city's signs. Where was he going? He seemed to be on his way somewhere. Where? Then it came to him, the hidden desire underneath the fragmented events of his day—he was going to Rose Davis's house. Not then, not that precise moment. He had just caught up with his own extended wish advancing before him. Now he must turn left and go home. The dog needed walking, and sometime tomorrow morning his own lawn would have to be watered.

CHAPTER TWO

Rose Davis stood in her front garden surveying what was left of it with a mixture of annoyance and disdain. She had been looking down at the choked lily pond, the silent fountains, and the dead leaves from her upstairs bedroom window for two months. Now she really had to do something about the grounds. The house had been her first concern. As no one had ever thought she might one day return, they hadn't bothered to keep it in the family. She'd had to buy the place back from an old couple anxious to retire to Florida. For the past few years they'd stayed downstairs in the living room and kitchen; what had originally been the dining room was their bedroom. Evidently they'd lived in the house like two moles going underground.

On taking possession she'd immediately opened all the doors and windows to rid the house of odors of gas fires burned too high, the dried leafy smell of the old man's pipe, and the dusty sweet perfume worn by the old lady. February first she'd let the cold rainy wind bang open doors and tear through halls. If she'd known any incantations she would have recited one for ridding the house of ghosts. Lacking a formula, she made up one of her own; she stood in the living room while the wind riffled peeling wallpaper and repeated silently, "Be gone. Be gone." Strands of paper rose and listlessly fell again like banners of a defeated army reminding her of the drooping flags around Napoleon's tomb. The sight of them always made her gloomy.

She began hiring helpers. The rest of the month, and through half of March, the rooms were crowded with termite exterminators, carpenters, painters, plumbers, electricians—so many workmen she'd begun to feel like a female Louis XIV bent on refurbishing her own petite Versailles. The house's various owners since her parents' death had perpetuated nothing but their own bad taste. She took pleasure in destroying all evidence of it. Now here she was in the wretched garden and, unlike Louis, she had no marvelous head-gardener. She supposed she'd have to find someone to help her, but that morning she'd decided she couldn't stand the sight of dead leaves any longer. Dressed in a faded blue cotton smock and armed with a rake the old couple must have forgotten in the garage, she stood on the broad front steps renewing her vigorous contempt for all those who had let the grounds deteriorate. *"Canaille,"* she muttered as she started down the steps to a corner of the yard dragging the rake behind her.

Because the yard was enclosed by a high stone wall, no part of it, except the oleander bushes and wisteria vines waving over the top, could be seen from the street. No one had to worry about keeping up appearances. She stopped to glare at the wisteria vine that had escaped its arbor on the side porch and taken off on a wild rampage through the treetops. Her father had planted that vine; she remembered sitting under a roof of lavender blossoms when she was a girl, a romantic idiotic young girl. Ah, well, she'd had a good time playing the fool waiting in a blossoming bower for another romantic fool to match her, and he never came. Rose smiled. In 1923 when she was only nineteen she'd married Edward Davis in a fit of impatience. Later she found the romantic fool in France. Silver-slippered, bead-strung, her youth flashed and was gone. Phillip, her only child, was born ten months after she married, and his daughter, Melrose, was in the back garden now priming canvas. She'd finish at the university, leave in May, and Rose wasn't sure what would happen then. The house was really too big for one person. Another, at least one other, would be needed. The grass looked remarkably green under the leaves. Putting aside future worries, Rose raked industriously for ten minutes.

For a moment she stopped to peer over the front wall. Her neighbor across the street, Mrs. Abercrombie, was out of town. The only people she'd met were the neighbors on either side; on the left was an Episcopal minister and his family, and on her right lived a rather reclusive lady, Miss Leila who, according to the number of empty bottles flung under the dividing hedges, sometimes drank too much sherry. The minister, Reverend Hallaran, had two children and one flop-eared hound with the appealing name of Grover.

The Hallaran children, a boy about seven and a little girl, Megan, approximately five, were riding their tricycles past her wall.

"An old witch lives there," said the boy.

"No, Mrs. Davis does. She gave me a orange yesterday. Daddy says there aren't any witches."

Head poked between oleander branches, hands clawing the top of the wall, Rose looked down on the children. She'd never been called a witch before. Sixty-three. Had she reached the age when "witch" was conferred? What age was that in this country now . . . whenever the wrinkles began to show? Perhaps she'd just forgotten to comb her hair that morning .

"See. There she is, stupid."

"Don't call me stupid!" The girl's voice rose in a piercing wail.

"Merde!" said Rose Davis to herself. She picked up the rake again, flung it down, and went to look for her granddaughter.

"Michael! Megan!" Mrs. Hallaran shouted for her children.

Rose could hear them arguing still as they went to their mother. On her side of the wall she walked across the side porch while the children straggled across their front lawn muttering to each other the unchanging threat of childhood, "I'm going to tell! I'm going to tell Mama what you said!"

She found Melrose in the back garden, her canvases spread in blinding white rectangles across the base of the wall fountain. The carved stone cherubs above the fountain seemed to be eyeing the canvases as if they were more promising, whiter clouds to abandon themselves to. Rose doubted if her granddaughter had noticed the cherubs. For an artist she had a remarkable number of blind spots. The child simply did not see much of the world, and what she did see was not forced through a fine sieve of abstractions and experiences, but concentrated and thrown like raw meat on canvas. Holding what looked like one of the house painter's fat brushes in one hand, Melrose was inspecting her priming job.

"They'll all have to have another coat."

How bright she was in the sun reflected from the canvas, her face flushed pink, her hair all yellow around it, how bright, and young, and energetic. She did not dawdle in arbors nor sigh over the white blossoms of the pear tree so quick to fall—and it was right behind her in the corner—she worked hard and patiently, waiting for no one. Rose envied her self-sufficiency while, at the same time, she marveled at it. She had known other artists and envied them in the same way. They made their own world, incomplete and imperfect but their own. She was, too many times, at the mercy of circumstance. She had gone to France on a whim, returned after seventeen years on another. Her friends thought she was decisive; she thought of herself as a drifter. Every move had been made, not for her own or anyone else's good; she had not chosen to do what was good, but what was appealing. Sometimes, accidentally, what was appealing was right.

The roar of a motorcycle approached the back gate and grew louder before it died. Beasts, lions and tigers together growling at the door to her jungle.

That would be George. She rather liked him. He was twenty-nine and did not seem be oppressed by questions about who he was or what he was to make of himself. There had been Conways in Austin ever since one of his great-grandfathers had moved to Texas from Tennessee. Melrose met him the year before at a kite-flying contest out in Zilker Park when their kites tangled. Melrose still had the one she'd entered, a beautiful thing, an orange, yellow, rust and black monarch made of tissue paper and balsa wood dangling from the ceiling above her bed. It had fluttered and swooped in the erratic wind before coming to land on a strangely light-looking pyramid George was flying. He'd untangled them. Picturing them busy with the kites on a sunny windy day, Rose thought it was a satisfactory introduction for an architect and an artist. George had already finished school. Now he was finishing his three-year apprenticeship.

"It's your beau," she said.

Melrose pinched her lips into an imitation of a bee-stung pout. "Rosie, it's only George. Nobody has beaux these days."

"Very well, Mademoiselle, your lover awaits at the gate."

Melrose put the back of her hand on her forehead and fluttered her eyelids in a mock swoon.

"*Quel dommage!* The poor fellow," said Rose.

"*Tant pis!*" Melrose retorted.

They both laughed. The dialogue of ironic insult was a favorite joke between them.

"*Voilà!*" George threw the door open. With both arms out flung he posed theatrically in his old shirt and blue jeans, then after waving in Rose's direction, he ambled across the lawn to Melrose.

Rose was amused by George. Imaginative yet practical enough, he lived on a houseboat on Lake Austin. Someday—he was already sure—he'd give it up, but at present it suited him. He thought he might live in a number of houses. Right now, he admitted, he was fond of temporary shelters. She'd never known a young man in the least like him. The men she'd known in her youth were not half as free with girls—with anyone—as George was. Despite the "wild youth" label of the twenties, the boys she'd known were not particularly wild. Those who really rebelled left town to dissipate in larger places. Even then their pleasures were not those of free spirits, but those caged in rebellion—to drink when prohibition was the law, to chase girls of questionable reputation, to throw themselves fully clothed into strangers' swimming pools at dawn, and finally to grow up as stuffy as their fathers, stuffier in fact since they had to weather the Depression.

George, apparently, was finished with rebellion. He liked his work, and he seemed to know how to enjoy himself. Did he enjoy Melrose? She didn't want to know. She could not be responsible for the morality of another generation, an attitude her son did not understand. When Melrose came to live with her she'd told him, "She will be free to go and come as she pleases. I will not be a housemother."

Phillip, his saturnine good looks deepened by age, gave her the full benefit of his psychoanalytical method. He said, "Hmn," a murmur, tentatively questioning without judging.

Rose grinned at him. "I thought you believed in permissive child raising."

The mask broke. Phillip's forehead wrinkled with concern. "Of course I do. That idea has its limitations though. I deal all of the time with people whose parents were too authoritarian, but that doesn't mean I handle my own child the way I ought to. Possibly I've leaned too far the other way. People like me are sometimes at their worst with their own children."

"You worry too much," she said and winced inwardly because there was no way out of parental worry. Phillip wanted his child to turn out well just as his parents had wanted him to become a well-rounded man. Well-rounded, yes, that was the term they'd used when he was growing up. She and Edward had been fairly successful, yet she couldn't remember any formula they'd used to make him what he was. Long ago she'd decided Phillip himself had been in charge of becoming himself. After his early years she and Edward had little to do with the way he turned out. When he was fourteen he'd decided to be a doctor, and after his first two years in college he'd decided to become a psychiatrist.

"You know I care about what happens to Melrose," she reminded him.

"Oh, Mother! She's lived in an apartment for the last two years. We've never asked her exactly what she does every minute. You know about her boyfriend. George. George Conway."

"Yes. Well, there's no use playing the heavy father or the meddlesome grandmother now, is it?"

"No. You're right. This is a different generation though. She's been fully educated. She knows everything about sex, reproduction, birth control. To me she seems so terribly innocent still."

"Perhaps her innocence will last a few more months."

"Oh, Mother, I don't mind her moving in with you!"

Of course he did. He feared she was too worldly, too wickedly Parisian. In a way she was. If Melrose had consulted her, she would have advised her to sleep with George and a few others too before she married—as long as no babies resulted. Ah, no. She could not give such advice. It was only what she should have done before marrying Edward. If anyone had advised her when she was nineteen to make that experiment, she would have dismissed that person as an intolerable cynic. For a moment Rose considered telling Phillip she had no influence over his daughter, nor did she want any. All she wanted was companionship, someone beside herself in the house; she was alone now. She would be alone later. Fearful of arousing unwanted pity, she kept silent. Phillip went back to Dallas with his beautiful, sane, competent wife Marilyn. He returned to his office and his patients; Melrose stayed with her grandmother.

Now George was complaining. "I'm taking her out for a cruise on my houseboat, Rosie, and she's not even packed a lunch. I guess I'll have to fish for us. I don't ever seem to catch anything but perch. It'll take three or four for lunch, don't you think?" He sat down on the edge of the fountain. The cherubs hovered above his head as he leaned back slightly.

A living valentine, thought Rose, and he wasn't in the least aware of being one. The young overlooked so much; they couldn't see the richness as they walked through it, but who could see it all entirely? Perhaps too much realization was unbearable except to poets, and even poets had to be blind to the world sometime. How else could they capture a bit of it?

The house George had been working on was almost finished, and when it was, he'd take them out to see it. He'd designed a place on the lake for an older couple, their visiting children and grandchildren. It had been a challenge trying to please three generations. Rose liked his desire to please. It was a two story house with a sleeping porch upstairs which had been surprising to her. She'd come to believe that everything was air-conditioned in Texas.

"At the lake at night they can do without, especially with ceiling fans," George said. He liked old-fashioned methods, old-fashioned girls, Melrose said. He was always finding some wonderful old thing that could be used; flaking wooden shutters might become glass-topped coffee tables, a rusty gate turned into a bedstead, joists from old houses could be sawn into flooring for new ones. And some things, he believed, should remain exactly as they were. George's kitchen was equipped with a green depression glass juicer and his grandmother's hand-turned food grinder.

When Rose asked him about it he admitted to being fascinated with the grinder when he was little. "Grandmother used to make her own mixture of sausage, and all those red wormy looking pieces—"

"Aggh!" said Melrose. "Little boys! Now that he's grown, it must be my cooking he loves me for."

"Not yours, not your peanut butter sandwiches, your grandmother's cooking. Rosie, do you have any *oeufs in gélee*?"

"The *gélee* would all be melted by the time you got to the lake."

"I love your *oeufs in gélee*!" George flung his arm around her waist. He danced her through the garden in a wide circle under the pear tree singing, "*Oeufs* in glue. How I love your *oeufs* in glue."

We are all a little mad in the spring. Rose abandoned herself to George's gallop, to sunlight, and dizziness. He whirled her up to the fountain's edge where they both sat down.

"You're a nice girl, Rosie, but you've got no dignity."

"Can't help that. Never had much."

"And that granddaughter of yours— She's got no sense."

Melrose waved a paintbrush in his direction.

"Save the paint for the boat!"

Melrose dropped the brush on the grass. "Always looking for slavies . . . slavie cooks, slavie painters!"

"I'm saving one whole wall for your mural. Come with us, Rosie?"

She almost said yes. To be in the sun by the water all day— Delightful. No, she would only be in their way. Grandmothers needed to stay at home and enjoy their solitude sometimes, she supposed. Fond as she was of both of them, she wouldn't follow Melrose and George around.

"Go on." She dismissed them. "I'll come when you've finished the whole thing."

Melrose picked up the brush. A dribbled white trail followed her out of the garden. George forgot to shut the gate behind him. Rose could see them both astride his motorcycle. The motor's roar, a familiar noise in Parisian traffic, sounded barbaric in the American Sunday morning stillness. Carelessly perched behind George, Melrose stuck the handle of the paint brush in her back pocket and threw her arms around him as they careened off. Phillip would not approve of his daughter riding a motorcycle; Rose swallowed an impulse to shout, "Be careful!" With the war dragging on and on, and George threatened by the draft as all young men were, it would be terrible for him to lose his life in a motorcycle accident in town. And if anything happened to Melrose. . . . This worry came to mind every time they rode away together, still she couldn't bring herself to natter on about obvious dangers.

She wandered into the house and sat down at the grand piano. The only thing she'd asked of Edward, it had been in storage all the time she was in France. Picking up the volume of Schubert *etudes* she'd ordered, she leafed through it idly. It had arrived along with another volume the day before. She was glad she'd already gotten the piano tuned, that the mice hadn't eaten the felt, and that Edward, in his usual careful manner, had also sorted out the pieces of her mother's furniture and stored them with the piano. Phillip, she supposed, had all the old sheet music. She'd forgotten to ask him if he still played for his own pleasure at least. Perhaps Melrose knew.

She put the heavy book on the music rack and began playing, sight reading slowly at first. When she was a child she'd studied piano, memorizing pieces to dazzle parents at torturous recitals, looking forward only to the refreshments afterward . . . spice cake, Miss Ora served it in thin slices followed by iced tea heavily flavored with grated orange rind. She could remember the tastes and smells of these better than she could remember years of French cooking.

After Phillip's eighth birthday he began taking piano lessons, not with Miss Ora or anyone like her, but with a vivacious young married woman, Anne de Buvre Tomlin. Rose took her son to his lessons. Entranced by his teacher's abilities, she began studying again. It was Anne Tomlin's uncle, Thomas de Buvre, who'd kept her seventeen years in France.

Rose smiled to herself. She never sat down to play without tasting cinnamon, nutmeg, and cloves, and smelling them laced with the flavor of oranges. Thomas had laughed at her, saying Proust needed only a madeleine, while she needed something more, the spices of the Indies brought to a perverse continent in the way of the route to the Indies. She had laughed with him enjoying the revolutions of his mind, but she could not rest in ironies, had no visions of ships loaded with spices returning to a New World; her memory clung to Miss Ora's crystal cake plate and the tinkle of ice in tall glasses, to the taste of dry sherry Anne Tomlin served after Phillip's lessons, to white Burgundy, the first one she ever drank, in a small French restaurant where a thin band of mirrors around the walls reflected her head and Thomas de Buvre's. This reappeared to her quickly as a sliver of light flickering and disappeared just as quickly. Oh, what had they said to each other then? Why does memory fail at the most important points? Rose let her hands fall to her lap.

She hadn't gone to Europe with the intention of staying.

In 1950 when she was planning to join a tour to France, Anne had told her, "You must meet my French uncle. A charming man. My favorite relative. I will write to tell him you are coming."

"You mustn't bother. Poor thing! What would he do with one more tourist!"

"He's crazy for *les Americains.* Do see him. He loves to show Paris to visitors, and you can tell him all about me."

They arranged to meet on the terrace in front of Sacré Coeur. She walked that morning by herself up the winding streets of the Butte Montmartre. Already worn out with the tour that ritually killed every hour by schedule, she escaped the company of too many women and their bullying guides for a day to go alone to the terrace. She should never have agreed to travel with a group; she needed to make her way on her own wandering schedule, to stare at a picture in a museum for thirty minutes or for three if she pleased. Being goaded along from place to place roused her anger so she'd told the guide at the Louvre, "I'll take a cab back to the hotel when I'm ready. Please go on without me." Despite his nervous protests, she'd carried out her plan except she sat in the Tuileries by the famous fountain as long as she pleased first. Now, after her immersion in the city, she hungered for the hilltop view. Intoxicated by the animation of people on the sidewalks, the beautiful clutter of open-air markets, long hours of gazing at cathedral windows, long walks by the sinuous curve of the Seine, she moved through days of delicious frenzy and came to Montmartre hoping to be lulled by perspective. All of Paris was spread before her; she picked out familiar towers and domes and rested content against the parapet. No memories of her own country or any of her previous life confronted her. Once she'd arrived on the continent she had ceased to worry about Edward. Their lives had grown so separate, and now he was thousands of miles away on the other side of a mail slot. Infrequently she saw a letter-box that seemed to glare at her reproachfully. At the moment, Paris, silver-gray below green leaves, commanded her full attention. Largely unconscious of place before, she was now dominated by the city. Already she had determined to stay. Before Thomas de Buvre had walked across the square ignoring buses disgorging other tourists, coming unerringly to her, before he had chosen her, she had chosen Paris.

She had thought they would meet as two civilized people good-humouredly doing a favor for a mutual friend.

"How long will you be here?" It was the first question men usually asked women visiting Paris. She had been asked before and had said to them all, "I leave tomorrow," but to Thomas de Buvre she said, "I am thinking of staying." Was it because she had just decided, or was it because he asked? She was never sure. She had no thought of immediately accepting another man while in the act of leaving Edward.

He asked about Anne. They spoke of her briefly as they walked toward the church.

"Do you want to go inside?" He smiled. "I have lived here for years and have never seen the interior."

"Then let's go in."

When they entered the dark church she felt his eyes on her. She had intended to look at him then. Outside in the bright light she saw nothing but his angular face above hers; she had sensed the man. His deference covered urgency; beneath that tactful shield was immense vitality. She carefully avoided contact, holding her arm closely against her side so she would not brush his coat sleeve, not minding his scrutiny. Her body was still well-shaped, her face relatively unlined. At forty-five she didn't attempt to be anything more or less than she was.

By the altar they paused to turn to the windows, modern stained glass set in patterns that appeared to be Byzantine. Silently they turned away and walked on behind the altar. A mass was being said.

"I am Protestant, but I like the smell of incense," Thomas whispered.

Rose smiled. Edward would not have noticed the smell, and if she had pointed it out to him, he wouldn't have liked it. Incense was too mysterious to him, too foreign; he would have disdained it as popery. She smiled slightly as she remembered this ancient prejudice.

They descended the steps outside Sacré Coeur, and still Thomas was watching her. He put out a hand to stop a photographer from taking their picture. Years later she complained to him about this action; it would have pleased her to have a picture of their first meeting.

"I wanted privacy. I wanted to protect you. You were still married then." He smiled. "I did not know if it was a first meeting or last."

Not until they sat down at a table across from each other did she see him, a man about her own age, with lively questioning eyes, dark almost black hair turning gray above his ears, a wide mouth, a face that must have troubled many women. He was divorced. She showed him a picture of her son and her granddaughter. He had a daughter in Grenoble.

"You are staying?"

"Yes."

"Your husband?"

"He will stay in Texas, I suppose." She did not mention divorce, hadn't thought about it, had no idea concerning Edward's reactions although she did not expect he'd like the idea.

During the next few weeks Thomas helped her search for an apartment. Finding one in the middle of an acute housing shortage was nearly impossible. She wanted to live near St. Germain de Pres.

"Why? It is crowded with tourists every summer and students all winter."

"I'm still a tourist myself. I feel at home there. I like the quarter. Why do you object? I can find something close to your shop."

"The shop is one thing. My house is another. I think you will not find anything near the Rue de Seine. Stay with me. You could. It will be so much easier for both of us."

Three nights before she'd slept with him for the first time and afterward, she'd spent the night at his tall ancient house, a large apartment actually, made up of the second and third story.

He showed her the library which was also his dining room with a kitchen just beyond. She leaned back in her chair trying to translate the French titles of his books. On one of the walls there was a collection of Napoleonic campaign pictures, printed in Epinal in the early 1800s. The retreat from Moscow was particularly dramatic. Billowing smoke, the city burned in the background while a heroic looking Napoleon riding horseback in full dress uniform led the ragged remainder of the Grand Army trudging on foot through snow drifts.

"He doesn't seem to be in the least aware of the cold or his defeat," she said.

"Yes," said Thomas. "It is folk art actually. Sentimental, reminders of those battles long after they were over. Tourists love these. Fortunately a great many of them were printed."

They had stopped by to have an after dinner drink on their way back to Rose's hotel.

"I have plans to seduce you," he said.

She'd thought he might. "Aren't we supposed to be sitting in front of a fire sipping brandy?"

"Yes. I'm sure that's correct." He smiled. "Only we have just these small liqueurs, and it is not the season for fires."

She could have said no. He would have waited. Instead she only nodded.

Taking her hand, he led her upstairs to his room where a large double bed waited with its covers already turned down. In contrast to the book filled downstairs with its long oval table serving for library use as well as for dining, his bedroom was quite plain, a place to sleep in and to leave.

"You did have plans, didn't you?" Rose took off her jacket. She could see a full moon out of the top half of the long window. "Have you also told the moon to rise at just this hour?"

"Of course."

It had been cool, cooler in Thomas's house than it would have been inside of most American homes. She shivered slightly in her slip and shivered again when Thomas pulled the straps down, but it was a different kind of shiver.

It seemed they made love several times that night. She hadn't counted but remembered they both laughed at their greed. Later, when the moon had gone down and Thomas slept, she stared out the window scolding herself. "Now, look what you have done!" In the morning she feared she would feel that she was somehow owned by him simply because they had slept together. She had promised herself she would not be owned by anyone again; her sentiments would not govern her life. For a long time, especially since she married so young, she had wondered what it might be like to live alone, she decided, in spite of Thomas's wishes, she must.

He wasn't pleased; still he'd helped her. Through some friends of his she leased the apartment of a couple that were going abroad. It was on the Rue de l'Abbeye by St. Germain with back windows overlooking the garden next to Delacroix's old studio. Around the corner was the Place Furstenberg, and a few blocks past it was Thomas's print shop on the Rue de Seine. For the first two years she'd lived alone in Paris; for fifteen she lived with Thomas. Seventeen years after meeting him on the terrace they parted, Thomas's body on a train to Grenoble, she on a ship to America. After the first tears, she pushed her grief deep inside where it remained, a hidden bruise anyone might innocently brush against. When Phillip asked about Thomas, she ached within while calmly answering, "He died quickly of a heart attack." Even as she spoke, she saw the wretched train leaving the station and sniffed its smoke which would bear, to her, ever after the stinging smell of regret.

Placing her hands on the keys again, she played through the piece once more forcing both meeting and parting out of mind, concentrating instead on clarity and tone. In the midst of a phase, the heavy brass knocker thudded against the front door. She ignored it at first thinking it must be one of the Hallaran children wanting attention then realized neither one of them was tall enough to reach the knocker. She flapped the Shubert shut and got up to answer the door. Impatiently she flung it open to a man waiting like a small lost bird that had struggled to the safety of her porch from the wilderness of her garden. Theo Isaac inclined his head toward her. His hair had turned white, but he seemed to have all of it still.

"I should have called you first." The years had marked her, left lines around her eyes, softened her cheeks, her eyes were still that peculiar gray-green, her mouth and chin firm. Her hair, gray as his was white, curled around her forehead, was pushed behind her ears. Had she combed it that morning?

"It doesn't matter, Theo. If you'd called, you'd found me dressed a little less like a peasant . . . maybe. Come in."

There was no furniture in the living room but a sofa, a low table, and the piano. Accustomed to the clutter of his own house and the museum, he was dazzled by the white walls and barren floor. He blinked and hesitated

"Here." Rose indicated the sofa. "I've only been back since January. This is all I've managed to find to sit on so far."

"I would have come sooner. I didn't know you were here until your granddaughter appeared at the museum yesterday."

"May Dickens told me you were sometimes out there." Rose gave him a conspiratorial smile. "I ran into her at the grocery store."

"Ah . . . well, yes. I'm at the Ney only on Saturdays."

"I was sorry to hear about Kate. May told me." She rushed to get over it, knowing she should mention Kate's death and hating to have to. Fresh sympathy could renew grief, even though Kate had been dead for two years.

She couldn't imagine how she would feel in two years. Quieter perhaps, less raw. Certain deaths, perhaps, marked one more than others.

Theo nodded his acceptance. He didn't know if he should say anything about Edward. Surely she knew he'd died in 1965 also. "I miss her."

"Yes, I know you do."

She might be missing someone also, but not Edward, not after so many years. Who had left her? He checked himself, and she aided him by asking abruptly how he liked her granddaughter's paintings.

"I've only seen one." Again, he hesitated looking up at her. Amusement flickered in her eyes, the same glance she'd given him when she was a freshman history student sitting on the front row of his class. He had just come back to Texas from Cornell. 1922. Austin was a town then. His family and Rose's had known each other well. She was eighteen, he was twenty-five, seven years separating them. Now there were the same number of years, yet eighteen and twenty-five seemed so much further apart than sixty-three and seventy.

"She brought a picture of a flat tire out to the museum for a show. I thought it . . . a bit depressing."

"I've seen more than one. Most of them are awful. I tell her so, and she tells me I don't know what's going on in art. She says the avant-garde has moved to America. I suppose she's right."

"They're not doing the same thing in France?"

"Oh Theo, by now they probably are. I don't know. In the streets all I saw were sidewalk artists and students turning out cheap pretties . . . little scenes to sell to tourists. I used to go to the Jeu de Paume to see the Impressionists because they delighted me. And to the Museum of Modern Art too, so I wouldn't get petrified with age. It does petrify you—never being able to change, stuck with the same ideas, the same tastes. Some people do that, keep the same opinions until they're like comfortable old clothes. Maybe they're afraid of betraying themselves if they do change. Forgive me. I have too many opinions myself."

"You've come back to stay then?"

"I suppose. I don't know. I got tired of being a foreigner. In Paris I was more American than I am in America. Here I'm in danger of being more Parisian than I was in Paris."

"I always wanted to see France. I had a year abroad in England, but I never saw anything more of France than the inside of a hospital in 1918."

"You're like my son Phillip. He stopped in the middle of college to do his service, and all he got to see was the inside of supply depots 'till '45. Why don't you go to Europe now?"

"I'm seventy years old." There, it was done. He had reminded her; of course it was apparent, but she should know he was well aware of his age.

"You can still see!"

"Yes, but I'm used to rising at six, eating one egg and toast at seven, watching the news, reading the paper, paying my bills, doodling through the day . . . settled."

"You have no grandchildren? They're good for unsettling one."

"Five. Three in Mexico City right now, two in Palo Alto. They might as well be in Lapland." He pulled out his pocket-watch. "I should go."

"Stay. I'll give you some lunch. Melrose has gone out to the lake. I'll have to eat alone if you won't stay."

"Let me take you out to lunch." He had no idea he was going to invite her. What prompted him? Where did the words come from? Marveling at his boldness, he sat quite still waiting to hear what improbable idea he'd come up with would next.

"Some other time, Theo. I'm lazy today. If I go out I'll have to dress. Won't you stay?"

He stayed though he felt he shouldn't. He was boring her sitting there gabbing about his meager existence. Somehow, in Rose's bare house, he felt impoverished compared to her. She had lived more, felt more, learned more than he, and he had been the teacher. Had he been saying his lessons by rote—repeating himself for forty years? No, not so. He had learned also; only in the last few years he seemed to have contracted, shrunk. Did one's mind shrink also, like a little dried pea in a pod? While Rose was still in the kitchen, he shook his head and wondered if he'd heard it rattle.

They ate lunch on the side porch. Next to it, he noticed, the iris beds were choked. Obviously nothing had been done to the yard in years, then gazing up at the empty crossed poles above, he asked what had become of the wisteria.

"You remember that vine? How good of you. The murdering thing has gone off to kill the trees. I need a gardener to get this place under control. Do you know of one?"

"I think so. If I can't locate one for you, Tim can. He's the caretaker at the museum." He shifted his weight slightly in the low-slung canvas chair hoping it would not collapse under him. Rose was comfortably sprawled in hers. How did she manage? A bit of salad slid from his plate into his lap. Gingerly he picked lettuce off his good black trousers.

"I'm sorry. Let me get you a paper towel."

"No, it's all right." He dabbed at the oily spots with his napkin. "This suit needs cleaning anyway."

"Theo, tell me what has happened to some of the people we knew."

His hand shook a little as he put the plate on the floor. "They are all dead, or in rest homes, or with their children. A number stay by themselves in their own homes. I don't really know how many of the ones we both knew are left, probably not many."

"It can't be as bad as that."

He thought for a moment of their contemporaries. "Helen Abercrombie—she lives across the street from you. She goes over to Georgia every spring to see her daughter and complains about having to look after the girl the rest of the year. The girl must be all of forty-five by now. Emery Pruitt is in a nursing home. His children had to put him there. He kept wandering around town by himself looking for home, the house of his childhood perhaps. When they took him to what used to be his parents' house, he couldn't recognize it. Finally he couldn't recognize his own house . . . the place he'd lived in for thirty-five years. Kenneth Wilson died last week—emphysema." He waved a deprecating hand. "I won't continue. It'll only make you sad."

"Jerry Tynes . . . did he ever marry Lucy?"

"Yes, and he gave her a peculiar wedding gift, a twenty-two pistol. Three weeks after the ceremony she shot him in one arm and got a suspended sentence for it. Kate used to say she did it because he made her wait so long. I think there were other reasons."

"Probably . . . generally there are. Edward's second wife— What was she like, Theo?"

"Not a bit like you."

Rose threw back her head and laughed. "I should hope not!"

"She was a rich widow from Oklahoma."

"So I heard. He always liked rich women."

"This one was intent on dispersing her wealth. She was on every board for every charity in town. People used to say it wasn't a matter of keeping up with her, but of giving up with her. Annabel was most generous." He stopped. Rose had always been the talker, and he'd been gossiping like an old woman over a back fence. "I didn't mean to imply you weren't charitable."

"Well, I wasn't particularly. If people asked me for donations I gave. I can't say I made a career out of it. How else was she different?"

"Not as pretty, attractive but not as pretty as you." He felt like an idiot, old as he was, complimenting a woman. It was the truth though. Annabel Davis with her little fringe of dark hair curling on her forehead like Mamie Eisenhower's, and her button nose along with the lines on either side of her mouth, reminded him of a Pekinese dog. It was no use to mention the resemblance. Annabel had gone back to Oklahoma, and Rose was here. She didn't look like any sort of animal.

"She was," he commented with a thin smile, "predictable." Then he asked the question he'd had in mind when he came, "What did you do in France all those years?"

The minute he asked he was appalled. How could he be so blunt? Living alone had dulled him. He'd been too long in the company of his own thoughts. "I shouldn't have—" he began. Before he could apologize Rose was answering.

"I lived with a man I loved. When he died I came home. I couldn't bear the loneliness. As long as he was alive I shared his life, but when he died I had only my own."

Theo assented to this with a quick nod.

Rose wondered if he understood what she was actually saying—that all her life had been centered around men. First there was Edward, then their son Phillip, then Thomas, and now she had to do without, to be preoccupied with herself, which wasn't enough. Coming back to Texas had, at least, given her something to do.

"Being alone is tiresome," Theo said. "I talk out loud to the dog, and he's half deaf, so I guess I'm talking to hear a voice. You're lucky to have your granddaughter."

"I won't have her for long. She's finishing her degree in May. Then she's leaving for the west coast. I should have come back when she was younger if I really wanted to know her. It's difficult at this age. About all I can do is try to understand. She visited me in France when she was a child and again when she was sixteen. All those years in between though—"

A jet broke the sound barrier, and they both looked up at the white streak on the sky.

"I'll never get used to the noise, and I'm sure I'll never fly on one. When I go out to see my son in Palo Alto I go by train. Hah! I wonder what Fred Harvey would have thought if he'd known one day the Santa Fe would become the preferred transportation for cranky old men!"

With her eyes still on the fading vapor trail, Rose nodded. Then she looked away from him for a moment as if she might be trying to conceal a snap decision and said, "Why not come stay with me when Melrose leaves, Theo? I'll put a sign on the wall saying OLD FOLKS HOME, and we'll sit here and be cranky together."

"But, Rose—"

"I knew you'd say that. You're right of course, another scandal, and Phillip wouldn't like it. Well, Phillip has his life and I have mine. As for scandal, I'm afraid that would only apply to you. I'm already as black as I can be painted. Who's left to gossip about us anyway?" Rose put her plate down and clasped her hands in her lap. She looked pleased.

"May Dickens is left!"

"Poor thing, she hasn't had a good story to tell for a long time."

He should ask her to come and live with him, return the invitation, but he preferred the emptiness of her house. His was too full of memories. If he left he'd have to get rid of many things, some of Kate's things.

"We should think about it, Rose, both of us. You are very kind to ask, and generous, but you ought to decide if you really want an old man around."

"Well, I don't want a young gigolo!" She laughed at the look on his face. Theo was still easily shocked. "And I do not mean to inveigle you into marriage. I've been thinking of asking someone to come live with me. This house is big enough for several more people. I don't want just another old lady for company. Me and another woman my age— Oh, no. That could be worse than any old man! Most women get so particular about their kitchens. I suppose it's because the kitchen is the one place we've generally ruled."

Rose had already heard too many arguments ranging from the kinds of dish towels preferred to how much seasoning was required in a particular dish. Daily pettiness could spoil every day.

"Um . . . m," Theo answered. "Too many cooks. . . ."

"And every woman has her own way of running a house. Certain days are washdays and others aren't. Disagreements about how to fold sheets and the best kind of furniture polish can lead to stupid quarrels."

Theo doubted that men cared about household decisions that much, not the men of his generation anyway. He'd had to learn how to do the wash after Kate died, and as for cooking, he was always glad he didn't eat much anyway. He admitted neither of these to Rose.

"Maybe we could find some young people too."

She seemed excited and purposeful as if she were enjoying making plans for both of them.

"I . . . I don't know any young people here except a little Mexican boy I met at the museum yesterday, and he's probably got a family. I know he's got a younger sister."

"We'll find some. There must be some young people who need a room and attention. We could have a *menage a trois* or *a quatre*."

"I don't know—" He sat with his hands clasped in front of him, all locked up. The idea was so appealing, yet he couldn't say so.

"There's an apartment over the garage in back. We ought to get someone for it. Or, if you prefer, you could have it."

Impossible to voice any decision immediately. His life had drawn in so—the house, the grocery, his part time job at the museum on Saturdays. It had been wider when he was twenty-five and Rose was eighteen, when he was her professor. Now she seemed to be his teacher. Her life was less cramped, less hedged about with walls of custom. Even her house was larger.

"I must admit, Rose, I . . . I don't like apartments. I like porches, and trees, and gardens. I like grass even if I don't like to cut it. I don't like elevators and corridors, and those barren stretches of rugs that creep on and on through halls past doors with numbers on them. I don't mean yours would be like that. It's just that more and more are getting built lately. The population here has doubled. People are living on top of each other in nested boxes!" He never knew he hated apartment houses so much. What an opinionated old man he was becoming, or did his assurance surface because she was opposite him looking interested?

"I don't like apartments here much myself. In Paris it's often all anyone can afford." Rose got up and took his plate. "Let me get you some coffee."

She stepped lightly through the open door leaving him in an agitated state. It had been years since anyone had fixed his lunch or brought him coffee; this being waited on by a woman was so soothing, so delightful. Did she actually intend for him to come and stay, to live with her? And how? She said she didn't want a young gigolo. What about an old lover? Maybe she didn't expect anything. How could he say it? Rose, I may still be interested in— No! Rose, I think I still like women. No, that wasn't saying it either. Rose, we are not kin. That was obvious. Phillip would not possibly approve. His sons? His sons' wives? They were a long way away, yet they did visit him. Perhaps he should arrange to always visit them. He could keep his new address secret. No, he couldn't be so devious. His heart was thumping ridiculously. Could Rose hear it? Crossing his legs, he held himself together rigidly. In fear of blurting the wrong words, his tongue locked behind his teeth.

By the time he left he was full of self-derision. What was he? A Casper Milquetoast reduced to a sop by a woman's kindness. Worse than that—a snail all curled up inside himself. All he'd managed to say to Rose was, "I'll think about it." What kind of commitment had he made? None. Safe, forever playing it safe. And here he was crawling home, a giant snail creeping ever so slowly down the sidewalk trying to stay in the shade, making himself as inconspicuous as he could as usual.

Late afternoon sun hit his back. Shaking with frustration, he pulled off his suit coat and threw it over one arm while he crossed the street. A car honked, swerved to avoid him, and honked again. Theo stood in the middle of the street, his fist raised at the back of the speeding automobile. He half expected the Keystone Cops to thunder around the corner and flatten him, or a custard pie to come flying toward his face. He wished for Chaplin's insouciant cane. Lacking that he flung his coat over his other arm and slouched all the way to the curb as though he didn't care if he were a public nuisance.

CHAPTER THREE

A tie. Anyone could buy a tie. First he had to find a cab though. He rifled through the phone directory's yellow pages. Cabinets, Cable Splicing. Cabs—See Taxicabs, Cafes—See Restaurants. He would never understand the mind behind the yellow pages. There it was, a two and a bunch of ones. A child could remember it. A seventy-year-old man could forget it.

He called the cab to come pick him up at nine. He would go to one of the men's stores on Guadalupe St. across from the university. They catered mostly to students, however, the older shops he'd used in years past were downtown, farther away and some of them might not be there now. At any rate, it was a more expensive trip to make. Bending down, he scratched the top of Homer's head. Kate had named him. She'd named everything including both children, the oldest Theo, after him, but they called him Ted. And Kenneth, the youngest, after her uncle. He could see her standing in the kitchen doorway saying, "Theo, let's give our children family names. I like that tradition." Wearing a loose pink housecoat, its ties hanging by her sides, her cheeks rosy in the reflected light, she wavered a moment in his memory, then was gone. It was always like that. What he most wanted to retain vanished, and even more frustrating, he couldn't ever recapture the time before a particularly vivid moment or the time after. He might call up a specific moment again, but he could never recall anything more. Memory was a candle flame flickering, then blown out by a spiteful wind.

He went to their bedroom and put on his suit. The dog padded after him staring mournfully as he went to the closet to hang up his robe.

"It's all right. I won't be long."

The cabby honked just as he was knotting his old tie; he had no chance to inspect his clothes. Not until he was inside the store did Theo catch a glimpse of himself in a mirror. The oil spots from the salad he'd spilled yesterday gleamed wetly on the front of his trousers. Black as they were, they still showed stains. Black as a crow he looked and dinghy! Umph! Shaking his head in disgust, he turned to a round table where ties were laid in an over-lapping kaleidoscopic design and considered the wild flowered prints, silk stripes, polka dots. He'd not seen such a profusion of color and pattern since 1923 in London when he'd gone with Kate to Liberty Silk where a clerk unrolled bolt after bolt for her to examine. He saw them again tumbling down the counter, the bolts thudding softly, richly until the bare surface was covered with shining rivers of silk.

"Can I help you, sir?" The clerk came from back of the store toward him.

He kept his gaze on the ties and said, "I would like to see some suits. Summer suits."

"What size, sir?"

Theo coughed discreetly and let his eyes run over what seemed to be almost a hundred suits catalogued behind size numbers. Then he looked at the clerk again. The young man was wearing trousers without cuffs, a veritable flower garden on his tie, and a shirt marked with thin green stripes. He lifted his eyes and confessed, "I'm not sure. I haven't bought a suit in some time." Not since Kate's funeral when he'd worn the one he had on. He'd decided that morning he needed more clothes. Vanity? Yes. So much else was stripped away from a man—when vigor was gone, when so many of his friends were dead, when wrinkles clustered, why not indulge his vanity? As a history professor he'd dressed like all the other birds in the flock, and a colorless bunch they were too.

"You'd take a forty-two, I'd say." The clerk slid his hand between the racks pushing away all the other sizes as if they were offensive to him.

Theo bought three suits; a dark blue, a light gray, and a blue and white striped seersucker, he thought. Dacron and cotton, Gordon said. Gordon Tanner was working his way through school. His field was economics. He liked selling. His uncle owned the store. This biography was shuttled in between information about fabrics, wash-and-wear, drip-dry, wool blends, and fashions. College boys weren't wearing socks this year.

He also bought five shirts to go with his new suits. All of them were mixtures of something or other. He was particular about the collars. "I like them soft, not floppy though." Gordon displayed them against the suits slapping each folded shirt down authoritatively. One was blue. Theo accepted it. He selected five ties, stripes and small geometric prints. "No blooms. I draw the line at flowers. You're young enough for them, but I'm not, decidedly not."

Gordon laughed. Did he need socks, handkerchiefs? Would he like to know where to go to buy a swimming suit? Theo told him about an eighty-year-old friend who still went swimming in the frigid waters of Barton Springs, yet he declined information about swimming suits.

He paid his bill with a check, adamantly refusing to start a charge account. Since Kate's death he'd spent money only on groceries, household bills, occasional cabs, insurance, taxes, his yearly medical examinations, and a few things for his grandchildren. He had plenty of cash. Now he wondered at his carefulness. For years, especially when the boys were growing up, thrift was a necessity. Later it was a habit. Until today frugality was one of the ways of accepting loneliness—he'd gone on as before, looked after himself, and asked nothing from anyone else. Perhaps his self-sufficiency, a characteristic he might have admired too much, had added to his isolation.

He felt at least ten years younger when he left the store carrying two bulging sacks. His only regret was he couldn't have the suits until the tailor was finished with trouser alterations on Wednesday. When he got outside in the sun he glanced toward the clock on the university tower. It was almost noon. He started to a taxi stand on the corner. Light-hearted and a bit light-headed, he peered in a drugstore window full of white boxes with blue tops; a sign on top announced they would keep soda pop cool on picnics. How could they? They appeared to be made of paper. A screech from a transistor radio assaulted his ears, a primitive wail from an electric guitar. Would his grandchildren, growing up with such sounds, ever have to learn how to waltz? Could he teach them to? He stepped under the projecting awning of a women's shoe store with a window displaying rainbow-colored shoes. What color were Rose's shoes Sunday? He hadn't noticed then. He would notice next time. Waiting at the taxi stand he traced a diminutive waltz step on the pavement, an old man fidgeting, someone might have thought. Light-headed, hungry, and precariously joyful, he knew he was dancing on a street corner at high noon.

The dog nosed at the sacks then ran under a bed and stayed. He was too deaf to hear the paper crackling. Perhaps he smelled the clothes, smelled something new and fled. Everything else in the house was old. Theo coaxed him out with hamburger meat, fixed himself some lunch, and deviating from his usual schedule for the second time that day, went to his study to write to his sons. He ought to have tackled letters to them when he was fresher, but he was too jumpy to nap now anyway. Better to get the task off his mind and rest later.

Dear Ted,

I received your letter dated March 17, and am delighted to know your research is going well. As for the teaching, though it is, no doubt, a strain to lecture in another language, you are to be congratulated for attempting to do so. The year in Mexico will also be good for the children. They have probably learned a lot of Spanish by now.

My situation here remains much the same except an old friend Rose Davis has moved back here from France. You may not remember her. She has a son Phillip about your age. He's a psychiatrist in Dallas now, and his daughter is living with Rose until May when she graduates from college.

Theo stopped. Entangled in generations. Well, out with it!

When Melrose, the granddaughter, leaves I am going to live with Mrs. Davis. We are both old and both live in big empty houses. Hers is emptier than mine because she brought no furniture back from France. I will take a few pieces from here. If you and Margaret want any of this furniture, let me know, and I will have it shipped to Tulsa. It can be stored until you return. I will make the same offer to Kenneth and Sally. As I do not want to worry with renters, I will sell the house.

Let me hear from you as soon as time allows. My best to Margaret and the children.

Love,

Father

He read it through, carefully tore the letter into neat squares and began again, this time neglecting the amenities:

Dear Ted,

This is to let you know I'm selling the house and moving to an apartment in June. Write to me if you want any of the furniture, and I will have it shipped to Tulsa and stored there until your return. This place is far too large for one person. I'm weary of rattling around in it and tired of taking care of the yard.

My love to you, Margaret, and the children.

Father

He could be devious if he pleased, and after all, it was none of Ted's business who he lived with. Sociologist though he was, Ted was only forty-three; he would understand his moving in with Rose as an old man's folly. And Margaret might let her children call her by her first name, yet she was a wife.

He sent approximately the same letter to Kenneth and Sally in Palo Alto. Somehow it was easier to write Ted first; probably because he was the farthest away, the one least likely to interfere. He did not anticipate any repercussions. Both sons were university professors. Though both had their summers free, neither liked hauling their families back to Austin to simmer there in 100 degree heat. He'd gone to Tulsa to spend last Thanksgiving with Margaret and Ted and to Palo Alto for a surreal Christmas with Kenneth's family. When his mind was ready to accept Santa Clauses in bathing suits and the scent of roses in bloom, he'd arrived to find dark gray rain blowing across dark green hills and the acrid sour smell of soggy eucalyptus trees. He sat in front of a fire most of the time telling his two grandsons all he knew about cowboys and Indians. The damp wind and the boys' war whoops drove him back to Texas. Perhaps he would return for a visit in the summer. He certainly had a traveling wardrobe now, not that he could actually see himself hand washing his clothes; the drip-dry idea was ridiculous. The sound of anything dripping, faucet or suit, would keep him awake all night.

The week passed uneventfully as usual. Then he began to wonder if Rose's invitation was serious. Suppose she often said such things capriciously? Wednesday, unable to stand his own silence anymore, he called Rose. He remembered the laughter in her voice when she talked about the sign—OLD FOLKS HOME. He waited, all locked up still, knowing what he wanted and too scared to say so. It was easy to write the boys, easy to decide what to do, almost impossible to voice his decision. His existence had narrowed so.

First he practiced his acceptance aloud: "If I'm still

welcome, I'll move to your house when Melrose leaves." Then he phoned her.

"Of course you're welcome. I need someone here, Theo."

"I would like to share expenses, and you must charge me rent too. That's only fair."

"Why should you pay rent? The house is already paid for. You'll be staying in what would only be an empty room otherwise."

"Rose, I insist. It's a matter of pride."

"All right. But it's not like you were moving to an institution."

It took him ten minutes to calm her. Still that was easier than the conversation he had with Kenneth when he called from Palo Alto Thursday night.

"Dad, what's this about moving to an apartment all of a sudden? I thought you hated apartments."

"Yes . . . well." Though he could lie on paper, it was much more difficult on the phone.

"Well, why are you moving to one?"

"For all the reasons I told you and Ted." They had been conferring. He could almost hear the sound of Ted's voice coming through the wires from Mexico City to Palo Alto. "Did you get a strange letter from Dad about selling the house?" That's what he would have asked.

"Dad, are you feeling all right?"

"Except for creeping senility, I'm fine." Kenneth was inclined to pry.

"I've always liked that house." He was inclined to hold onto things too. Kate wanted to get rid of his rock collection when he went to college. None of them were identified or labeled. They were just rocks. Kenneth had insisted on putting them in boxes in the attic. They were still up there with his electric train, his old yearbooks, and a collection of all the letters he'd received from girls. Did Kenneth want him to remain as custodian? Was every old person required to run a private Smithsonian containing the relics of his children's past?

"I'll ship anything you want, but you'll have to take care of half of the charges." He had a welcome vision of movers heaving out boxes of rocks.

"No, Dad. I may want something, yes. I only meant I liked the house."

"I'm tired of it. I intend to move."

"Have you picked out an apartment? Can we help you? Sally says she'll come to Austin and —"

"I appreciate the offer, Kenneth, but Sally has enough to do. I can find an apartment. I'm looking for one now, and I can move. I'm not feeble. I'm just a little slow." He laughed. He was almost beginning to enjoy himself.

"Well, we thought being uprooted might—"

"I'm not being uprooted. I'm transplanting myself and in the same town I've lived in for most of my life." What he really needed to say to his son finally came to him. "Don't worry, Kenneth. Even old people need a change. I'm just providing myself with one."

Theo put the receiver down, heard a gratifying final click and said to the night, "Whoosh!" Turning slowly around, he stopped the swivel chair, stood up, and moved across the room while unconsciously humming *Tea for Two.* Then he heard himself and for the second time that night, he laughed aloud. Waltzing alone again!

Saturday he wore his new gray suit to the museum. Ricardo was waiting for him on the front portico and followed him inside as soon as he opened the door.

"My father says I should come with him, but I don't this morning."

"Where was your father going?" Theo turned on the lights in the north studio.

"He goes to cut grass for people. I help him some."

"Your father does yard work?"

The boy tensed his hands into fists and hit them together. "You got a yard?"

"I've got a friend, a lady, who needs help with her garden. There are fountains and all sorts of flowers, and no one has cared for them in a long time."

"Are fish in the fountains?"

"I don't know. I haven't looked."

"Goldfishes eat mosquitoes."

"Do they?" How many things he didn't know still, how much Ricardo already knew—Spanish as well as English, the way all over town on a bicycle, how to rid pools of mosquitoes.

"Every fountain must have goldfishes. Next Saturday I bring my father and the fishes. OK?"

"All right." Theo gave him Rose's address. "I can't be there as I have to come to the museum, but you'll like Mrs. Davis."

"I like the flowers. I don't like the grass."

"Well, you can't have all flowers." Theo turned to go upstairs and check on the latest abominations that had arrived for the art show. He was stopped by a shout from Tim in the back. What was he saying? Was it a complaint of some kind?

Tim waited with his hands on his hips before a large crate. "Look here. I got this thing to undo, and it says *Glass Fragile* all over it— Say, you got a new suit." He laid his hammer on top of the box and came over to him. "That's sure a good looking suit."

Theo thanked him. Foolish how a little praise from Tim made him feel so good. One new suit or three didn't make him a new person, yet praise from a kind-hearted man gave him an almost childish pleasure.

"And a new tie too!"

Tim grinned then began prying nails out of one side of the crate. Ricardo stepped around him to the opposite side.

"You hold it steady now, and we'll find out what's in here."

Theo left to turn on the lights in the west studio. Overcast as it was that morning the figures all took on a ghostly appearance, especially Lady MacBeth wringing her hands in mid-air. Miss Ney had frozen her in the "All the perfumes of Arabia will not sweeten this little hand" scene. It wasn't a bad idea to try, but under bright light her permanent anguish seemed overwrought.

She and Prometheus were the only literary characters Ney had attempted. Fredrich Wöehler, prominently displayed on the mantelpiece, gazed indifferently toward the tortured lady. A German chemist, he had been one of Elisabet Ney's best known works. How he had discovered her, or exactly how the Munich Polytechnic Institute had chosen her to sculpt his head or how the cast of Wöehler's head arrived in Texas, Theo didn't know. He marveled at the ability of anyone to discover anyone. The tenuous strands connecting one person to another, how insubstantial they were, yet how tough and elastic. He had known Rose's parents, had her briefly for a student, admired her beauty and her spirit, supposed she was gone forever, found her again though her granddaughter and May Dickens. Gossips served their purpose.

"Mr. Isaac, come see what we got!" Ricardo was calling.

"It's a box, a glass box with a pink man dancing. You got to come see."

He didn't think he wanted to, but Ricardo kept insisting so he went out to them.

Tim was laughing. "I don't know. I don't know why he—"

Ricardo jumping up and down as excited as if it was a gift for him he'd just opened.

A square glass box firmly attacked to an iron stand and on two sides pictures of a black man—pink. At right angles on the other two sides the man was reflected in bright green. Theo didn't know what to think. He'd never confronted anything like it. At first he could only wonder how the box had been constructed, how the prints had been made on the glass.

"Whoo-ee!" Tim shook with laughter. "That fellow's color blind all right." He was sitting on part of the crate, his head thrown back.

"I like the colors," Ricardo said.

"So do I, boy!"

Theo stopped frowning over the box and looked at the black man in his white jacket, white on black, the Mexican child's yellow tee shirt against his light brown skin, himself, gray suit on white. Then he looked again at the pink and green black man dancing. It didn't matter. Their color didn't. He had never believed it would matter in the end, someday after all the suffering was over, when the wars were fought, the marches finished. Sometime . . . years after he was gone, a man's color would no longer determine his freedom. But this artist broke the barriers now, broke them laughing.

"He managed to get it here just in time. They will judge the pictures this afternoon."

"Do you think he'll win?" Tim asked.

Theo agreed that *Man Dancing* should win although he knew he should be backing Melrose's picture. Unfortunately hers continued to depress him. He and Ricardo stayed past closing hours that afternoon waiting for the jury to decide. They promised to call Tim. There was only one problem; Tim said his phone was "on vacation" which meant he hadn't been able to pay his bill. The phone went on vacation often.

"You can call next door. Those people will get hold of me."

Theo started to offer to pay Tim's bill then checked himself. He'd offered before, and Tim said he'd rather owe Bell Telephone than anyone he knew.

The jury arrived at five and spent an hour and forty-five minutes making up their minds. There were three judges; a young man from the art department of a nearby Catholic college, a woman painter of some distinction who lived in Austin, and a museum director from San Antonio. Theo would have liked to have heard every word they said. The temptation to eavesdrop was so great he confined himself to Miss Ney's old kitchen in the basement where he made a cup of tea. As soon as his cup was ready he escaped into the adjoining dining room. Perhaps it was cheerful when a fire was burning. It was rather dreadful being alone at the huge table. Stone walls with tiny barred windows at ground level might have made Miss Ney feel safe. He felt imprisoned and was glad Ricardo kept running down from his post at the bottom of the stairwell to repeat muddled phrases and impressions.

"Somebody, the San Antonio man, I think, says, 'Not much!' The lady says she likes the old tire. The other man walks around and around."

Theo sighed. He was as impatient as Ricardo. They met the jury at the bottom of the stairs. *Man Dancing* won first, Melrose's picture second, and a still life of some lemons was chosen third.

When Theo called Melrose, she wasn't bothered by second place, nor was she excited by the prize. "It's good to have. It won't mean much anywhere else though."

Then they dialed Tim's neighbor who went to get him. When he came to the phone he spoke first to Ricardo who reported, "He says he don't believe us. I told him *Man Dancing* won, and he says, 'How could a pink nigger win?'"

"Ricardo's right, Tim." Theo shouted then took the receiver. "He's right. It did win."

"How much does it cost? I wish I could remember. I never saw a picture I wanted to buy in my life, but I sure would like to buy that one."

"Three hundred and fifty dollars, I think."

"Humph! That's more than I owe Bell Telephone."

"Perhaps the museum will buy it. Sometimes galleries keep permanent collections of pictures just as we have Miss Ney's things."

"Well, it's her place. I don't see no pink and green black men getting in there for good." Tim's voice was mournful.

"You can never tell what they'll decide to do here next."

"That's true."

Before he left Theo put an envelope containing a check for $350 and a note saying he wished to remain anonymous in *VOLUNTARY CONTRIBUTIONS.* On the outside he typed: For The Museum's Purchase of *Man Dancing*. He did it for himself as much as for Tim. It was particularly satisfying to be an anonymous benefactor. It would have been more practical to give Tim the money. He wouldn't have taken it as a gift and if he had, his conscience and his wife wouldn't have allowed him to spend it on a picture. Three hundred and fifty dollars would have gone to the telephone company, to doctors, to department stores. He and Tim needed the picture more than any of those people needed their money. It was the first modern thing that either one of them had liked. He debated about telling Rose and decided against it. Better to remain completely anonymous, to have a private joy, much more rewarding than private sorrow.

He would see her that evening. *My Fair Lady* was showing at one of the theaters near the university and within easy walking distance of her house. It was her idea, the first time she'd been to a movie since returning to the states. He couldn't remember the last time he'd been. He used to take Kate to musicals. She liked them. He didn't particularly because most of them seemed vapid. Since *My Fair Lady* was based on one of Shaw's plays it should contain enough of the original vitriol to be amusing.

He found he'd worried needlessly about amusing Rose. As a returned expatriate she found novelties everywhere. After years of walking about Paris she could not make up her mind if she missed the surge of traffic or not.

"It's so calm! was her first reaction. Then, "Maybe it's too calm. I miss the feeling of achievement after crossing a street."

They cut through a small park near her house and she wondered at the lack of chairs. Twilight drew in around them.

"It doesn't last long here. I'd forgotten. In Paris the spring and summer evenings are much longer. There's no gabble of conversation in the streets, only me complaining like the French do when they're in another country. Oh, I have become hard to please!"

Walking down Guadalupe she could not help but notice that houses had been replaced by cheap restaurants and small businesses. A giant figure of a man in a red shirt and blue trousers, his feet planted wide apart, glared at them from the roof of an open-walled shed. A sign stuck in the asphalt read *CAR WASH* $1.00. The man, twice as high as the building he straddled, had a square-jawed smile more forbidding than beckoning.

"Even if I had a car I'd never drive it in there!" She tilted her head back and stared up. "He makes me feel like a pigmy! Isn't that the most terrible smile!"

"Yes, but you should see some of the other figures around town. There's a monstrous termite that revolves twenty feet above the corner of Enfield and Lamar, and out on South Congress there's a hamburger three times bigger than both of us. It's a kind of balloon, filled with helium, I suppose. Every time I go past it I hope a small boy with a B-B gun will use it for a target." Ricardo might do it. No, it wasn't a thing to suggest to a child, destruction of property. English common law had made respect for private property a virtue, and Adam Smith had justified free enterprise by defining it. No point in taking up a B-B gun against all that. He sighed quietly. Rose heard him anyway.

"Why, Theo, what's the matter?"

"I was thinking, if I were a benevolent dictator, I'd— Oh, I don't know. I was thinking I might send out bands of young boys to shoot holes in things . . . a sort of old grouch's program."

The light changed, and they crossed the street. When they reached the sidewalk he continued, "No, it wouldn't be right, satisfying a personal prejudice. If I were really benevolent I'd try to get us out of Vietnam first."

"Hah! Some of my French friends said, 'We understand the American position. We fought that war a long time too.' Others said, 'You're wasting your time in Asia. You'll know it when you've been there as long as we were.'"

"To one I said, 'You are probably the only ones who understand.' I told the others, 'No doubt you are right.' Neither group wanted to know what an American really thought. They might have backed down if I'd put up an argument. There's nothing the French love so well as someone who'll fight, but I didn't have the heart for it. The ones who said we were wasting time were right . . . only we're wasting so much more—all those lives."

"If you had told them we are fighting a war they should have finished, or that their own government in Vietnam was hopelessly mismanaged—"

"I would have been insulting them. They were already embittered by the Algerian war. I lived through most of the Fourth Republic and the return of DeGaulle. I couldn't help but think of him as a nation saver. Generally I'm in a muddle about politics. Thomas used to try to comfort me by saying no one made as great a muddle as the French. He was in England during most of World War II as a member of DeGaulle's army. Sometimes his point of view was rather English." The first time she'd said his name aloud to Theo. It had to be mentioned eventually. Why had she chosen to talk about Thomas while walking on the street? She watched the cars for a moment thinking, as she usually did, how large American automobiles looked after seeing Citroens, Renaults, and Volkswagens for so long. Thomas. Talking about Thomas. Maybe it was because they had been talking about politics. No matter. I have to say something about him now and then. There's no canceling out those years, and I don't want to. I will not cry in public. I will not.

Theo watched her blink her eyelids rapidly. Thomas . . . so that was his name. Go ahead. I don't mind if you cry. I am familiar with grief. It takes you at the strangest times, with no warning. You can be slicing bread in your own kitchen or walking down a street. Memory keeps no hours.

Rose refused to cry. She looked over at him and said in her normal voice, "I'm sure I'm insufferable, complaining about America so. Some days I think I have too much to remember."

Theo smiled. "Better too many than too few."

The entrance to the theater was flooded with light. Posters advertising *My Fair Lady* promised song, dance, romance while intimating gaiety, renewal, forgetfulness. They submitted to all these illusions willingly. Theo, collecting his change from the ticket seller, looked down at Rose's shoes beside his. They were pink, pink as the flowering peach blossoms in bloom. Yes, of course, they matched her dress. What marvelous frivolity! Forgetting his timidity, he took her arm and guided her through the door to the lobby as if he were leading her into a grand ballroom.

"Dad?" Kenneth seemed to be speaking to him from the Sunday morning editorial page, which he always read thoroughly. Theo preferred editorials to preachers. Too much Sunday school in his youth, he supposed. Though he'd gone with her now and then, Kate had been the churchgoer.

"I'm here . . . in the dining room."

The dog growled belatedly.

"Hush, Homer! A lot of use you are." Theo whispered. All the china he'd gotten out to pack was stacked on the opposite side of the table. Kate's mother's Haviland, her own pre-war Bavarian, sets of twelve of both patterns were piled in front of him. There were a few cups missing. Which one would want what? Would they quarrel? He hoped not. Maybe Kenneth, now that he'd arrived, could decide on— What was he doing here?

"I see you're serious about this move." Kenneth shook his father's hand.

Theo reached up and patted him on the back. "Sit down. There's coffee."

"No, thank you. That's about all they give you these days on planes."

"And Sally—?" He knew Kenneth had come alone. He looked too much like a man off on a mission to have brought anyone with him.

"Oh, she's at home . . . fine. She and the boys send their love."

He sat down, unconsciously choosing the chair he'd used as a child.

Theo wiped his mouth carefully as he studied his youngest son. Trim, keeps himself in shape playing tennis, an associate professor of English, likely a full professor in a few more years, an eighteenth-century specialist, forty-five but thinks he's my father. He poured himself another cup of coffee and wondered how he was going to escape the burden of his son's concern.

"Would you like to pick out some china?"

"No. That can wait. I've got to get back to classes by Tuesday, Dad. This is really a quick trip. I need to catch another plane out tomorrow. I want to see where you're going to live."

Moving around that fast wasn't good for anyone, Theo believed yet kept quiet. Kenneth's pace was his business. And where he lived was no one's business.

"Why are you so curious?"

"I don't understand why you've changed your mind so quickly. Why do you want to leave this house?"

"Kenneth!" Theo stood up. "Since your mother died, this house has become a grief to me. At first it was a solace . . . someplace we'd shared. Now it's only a reminder of my loneliness." He spread his palms deliberately on the table to soothe himself.

"You could come to us."

"You are kind to remind me. I remember you've invited me before. Everyone wants his own way of life all along. Maybe we want it even more as we get older. Surely you understand that."

"What are you saying, Dad?"

He glared at Kenneth seeing Kate's fair hair, her blue eyes, and at the same moment he saw a ten-year-old boy, his pockets full of marbles, waiting to be excused from the table.

"Never mind."

He left Kenneth on the porch with the paper while he washed his dishes and marveled at his delaying tactics. When he was drying a cup for the second time, Rose called.

"I'm going out to the lake, to Lake Travis, with Melrose to look at George's houseboat. He's gone to Kerrville to see his parents this weekend. Would you like to go with us?" The sound of her voice was so welcome he smiled at the phone receiver.

"I can't. My son Kenneth is here. He's just arrived from California. I didn't even know he was coming."

"Checking on you, isn't he? Why don't you bring him around later this afternoon? We'll be back by five."

"Would you like for me to?"

"Certainly, Theo. What does he drink, martinis?"

"I don't know." He smiled again. How like Rose to worry about what she should give anyone to drink. "I don't know what any of them drink anymore."

"That's a good reason for martinis. I'll see you and Kenneth at five, Theo."

Immensely relieved, he went to look for his son. The paper covered Kenneth's face. He'd taken off his jacket and tie. One foot was propped on the porch railing. The rocking chair tilted forward as the screen door closed.

"Now you see what happens to old men on Sundays."

Kenneth slid the paper away from his eyes. "It's a long flight back here. I never can sleep on planes on my way anywhere . . . only on my way home to California."

"Wouldn't you like to go upstairs and take a short nap?"

"I thought we ought to look at places—"

"I . . . I have one in mind. I'll show you this afternoon."

Kenneth handed the paper to him and went indoors. Theo heard his footsteps on the stairs. Going up to sleep in his room. He can sleep there again tonight for the last time, but he doesn't believe that yet, thank God.

Rose peered at the side of George's boat. What had Melrose done? A green monster writhed on the wall, not a playful Disney dragon but a ferocious Chinese type, fire-breathing, tail-lashing. The wings were outlined though they weren't painted in yet. She glanced back at her granddaughter waiting on the path above.

"George's house is safe from dragons."

"I hope so. This is his only one. He believes architects should try all types of houses."

"Does everyone in his firm have a different kind?"

"He's quitting the firm at the first of the year. He'll be on his own, Rosie. Freelancing. As soon as he's finished the boat he'll move here to live year round. It's cheaper and more fun."

"And in the winter? If I remember correctly, it gets pretty cold sometimes." Rose pulled off her sandals and dangled her feet in the water. They looked so white, too white, like fish bellies.

"He says he's waiting to see about the winter. He also says I should stay here and keep him warm." Melrose leaned against the dragon's mouth just at the point where the fire rushed out.

With her long blonde hair and pale coloring, she looked a bit like a heroine in an old melodrama. Blue jeans and an orange tee shirt ruined the effect somewhat; still she could see why George wanted to keep her there. Other men would want her to stay in other places.

Rose went on paddling her feet in the water and kept quiet. Sometimes she felt she'd perfected the art of holding her tongue. Here she was, a wonderful example of someone who'd married too young. She had no business giving advice. George certainly wasn't Edward Davis all over again. That was one good reason for keeping her thoughts to herself.

"I like the dragon."

"Do you? It's not what George would call organic. Just decoration. I need some gold paint for the wings. I want them to shine."

The dragon was from Grant Avenue, San Francisco. She was already half-way there, half-way away from Austin. "You want to leave, don't you?"

"Yes. George may live in a houseboat, but he's got all sorts of ambitions. He's older, ready to settle. I can love him without marrying him. You did that." Melrose sat down beside her and put her feet in the water without taking off her tennis shoes which Rose thought was odd, however she seldom commented on Melrose's habits.

"I liked Thomas. He was wonderful to me that first summer I came over. I was so crazy about puppets. He took me to all those puppet shows in the Luxembourg Gardens."

"He wanted you to like him. He planned for your enjoyment.

I used to think sometimes I might be jealous." Staring at the sheet of water sparkling before her, Rose remembered the deepness, the darkness, of the Jardins du Luxembourg. Anything might be hidden there; anything might quickly spring to light in its formal open spaces.

"Grandpa Davis was jealous!"

"How could you have known that? You were only a child at the time, nine, I believe."

"He gave me a horse when I came back that fall. It caused a lot of trouble. It was a quarter horse, and I was dying to learn to ride English style like those elegant people I'd seen in the Bois. Thomas took me there. Do you remember?"

Wind rippled the water; a cluster of dark purple winecups, some of the first spring wildflowers, shook their heads as though deploring human passions.

Rose nodded. On this lake shore in the middle of Texas she could see Thomas striding toward them over the hill in his polished boots, cream colored jodhpurs, a silk cravat tucked under his open collar.

"You bought me English boots, jodhpurs, a jacket, and a black velvet riding cap. None of those matched Grandpa Davis' horse. We took it to Dallas and put it in a stable. After about six months Mother and Daddy let me trade it for a thoroughbred."

"Was your grandfather angry?" Even though she'd left him, Rose was still genuinely curious about her ex-husband. Old marital loyalty mixed with anger at his rigidity and weariness with her own stifled patience, which led her to put up with everything too long, faded after she met Thomas.

"I thought he would be. He was more interested in the details of the trade than anything else. I think he was proud I'd managed it. He was indulgent. So was Thomas, but he wasn't a grandfather . . . I didn't think of him as—"

"I'd decided I wouldn't marry again." Rose pulled her feet out of the water and lay down on the warm boards of the dock. "I was contrary and difficult, and I can't even say I did the right thing. He wouldn't come over here, not even for a visit, unless we married first, so we didn't come. He used to love to hear you talk about the wild west."

"Sometimes I was too aware of him listening. I mean if I talked about Grandpa Davis's ranch, I had to call it 'the ranch near Austin,' not 'Grandpa's ranch.' I'd start talking about the deer, or the doves shot that season, how dry the summers were, the colts born in the spring, and before I knew it, I'd be mentioning the swimming pool they were digging in front of the house. Grandpa and Annabel were always 'they.' Mother and Daddy were the only members of the family I could call by name. He listened so closely."

"Yes. He wanted to know about those family relationships you wouldn't mention. Often I had to fill in the blank places later for him."

Melrose laughed. "I was too careful, wasn't I!" She ran one hand over a board, gathered her fingers together, spread them apart again. "George wants to get married, and I don't." Pulling her feet out of the water, she let her shoes drip a minute before she began stomping back uphill to her car. Rose, listening to the squish of water in tennis shoes, followed her wet footsteps.

"Whose house is this?" Kenneth asked. They were standing at the front door, the fishpond, a dark rectangle outlined with splotches of green lily pads, behind them.

"It's Rose Davis's. She's an old friend. You might know her son. He's a few years younger than you. Phillip. Lives in Dallas. He's a psychiatrist. His daughter lives with Rose but she's leaving in May. When she moves out, I'm moving in."

At the precise moment he finished his announcement, Theo let the heavy knocker thud against the door. Rose opened it before Kenneth could say anything more than "Oh?"

"Come in. Do come in, Theo." She took both of Kenneth's hands. "You resemble your mother, a lovely woman. I admired her. Let's go sit on the side porch. I haven't collected enough furniture for this room yet."

Kenneth's disapproving eyes passed over the grand piano, the couch, the table.

"I plan to contribute a chair," said Theo blandly.

Rose said, "How do you feel about martinis?"

"Oh, fine, just fine. Can I help you?"

"When you see my cocktail shaker, you're going to think I need help." She disappeared into the kitchen and when she came out again carrying a tray with a teapot and three glasses on it, Theo noticed she was barefooted. Her long full skirt hid her feet part of the time. Perhaps that was why he hadn't noticed before. Perhaps she'd merely forgotten to put her shoes on.

"I have been moving, Kenneth. My possessions have dwindled." She swirled the teapot about with one hand while holding its top with the other, poured the martinis quickly and raised her glass, "To your health."

Kenneth took a large swallow.

"I've been living in France so long. Tell me about California now. Is it still the trend-setting state?"

"Oh, yes, in the worst way. Everything erupts there. Student riots, drugs, smog, population explosions, earthquakes. Of course in Northern California we tend to get a little smug. We believe all the worst things begin in the south. It's the geographic theory of disaster. When you've gone as far west as you can go, you look to another part of the same state to blame for all your troubles."

Rose felt under her chair and pulled out a pair of sandals. She smiled as she put them on. "Having someone else to blame is a great necessity."

She led him to talk about his teaching, his students, his interest in the eighteenth-century novel. Listening to her, Theo was as beguiled as if she had been speaking directly to him. Gradually Kenneth began enjoying himself and forgot to be dutiful. Halfway through his drink Theo forgot his own caution. He liked watching his son, liked listening to his measured answers, and was surprised, as always, at some of the things he said. Kenneth and Sally were planning a move themselves. It was time for them to have a larger house just when his father wanted half of one.

"Rose, I've told my son I'm coming to live with you toward the end of May."

"Ah." She turned back to Kenneth. "I look forward to having your father here. We're good friends. It seems so much more sensible to share a house rather than live apart in two large ones. I don't like living alone. For a period in my life I tried it but not for long. I've grown used to having someone around."

"Of course. We all do."

He seemed to have forgotten, for the moment, that his childhood home was going to be sold. As they passed the lily pond on their way out, he put one hand on his father's shoulder and whispered, "She's a dear."

"I know. I'm a lucky old man."

The iron gates creaked shut. Theo turned back to check the latch.

"Have you thought of marrying again?"

"Rose has told me she isn't searching for a husband."

"Maybe she'll change her mind."

"Kenneth, before you get my future completely planned, could we go eat supper?"

"I'm glad," Melrose said, "you're coming to stay with Rosie. I was afraid she'd be lonely when I left." It was intermission at the Monday night concert. They were standing against the wall of the lobby in the Music Building at the university. Over Melrose's shoulder Theo could see May Dickens bearing down on them. He exchanged glances with Rose and decided he'd let her do the talking.

"Theo! Rose! I'm so happy to see you two here." May sputtered to a stop in front of them. She was a small fat woman with dark eyes and tight gray curls bobbing like little springs all over her head. No matter how still she stood she always appeared to be in motion.

"I told you, Theo, you were missing something by not coming over here. Wasn't the Handel divine! Rose, how did you get him out? He's been hibernating like an old bear." She wiggled her finger at him.

Theo restrained an impulse to catch it and see if he could hold her still. No, he warned himself, it would be like touching a mobile; some other part of her would begin jiggling.

"I don't believe you've met my granddaughter," Rose said smoothly.

Melrose said hello and introduced George who spent the next five minutes saying yes he was Frank Conway's son, and his father and mother now lived in Kerrville because the summers were so much more pleasant for them there.

"You can have my room," said Melrose. "It's upstairs in the trees."

"Shh!" Theo whispered.

May turned toward him just as he inclined his head in her direction. He couldn't tell if she'd heard Melrose or not.

"What's this? Are you moving, Theo?"

He looked at her and smiled without answering, hoping she would think he hadn't heard. A polite way of saying it's none of your business might occur to him if he had a minute.

"Anne!" said Rose. "I thought you might be here."

Theo, silently blessing this intervention, smiled broadly.

Anne Tomlin leaned over to give Rose a kiss. "You're looking beautiful. Isn't she?"

Theo nodded. Anne Tomlin, as he remembered, was a beauty herself. In middle age she retained her animation, and her eager interest in others warmed everyone around her..

"Claus is backstage now. He'll want to see you."

"Anne's husband is the conductor," Rose explained. "Come and bring him over to the house for a drink when this is over. You must meet him, Theo."

Theo nodded again. May, he could see, was still waiting for a chance to ask more personal questions. He couldn't give Anne his full attention no matter how much he wanted to. He pretended he saw someone he knew and moved away a little. On his left he could still hear May expertly probing Melrose about her plans for the summer. George rolled his eyes toward the ceiling then drew May away by the arm as if he had something terribly important to confide. Holding onto her elbow, he steered her deferentially through the doors and back to her seat. When he joined his party once more he leaned over Melrose and winked at Theo. Mendelssohn's music to *A Midsummer Night's Dream* was beginning; it would end with *The Wedding March*. Theo, daunted by a sudden need to avoid public announcement of his move, had no heart for the ironies of Shakespeare's fantasy such music would bring to mind. From several rows behind he could feel May Dickens's hard little eyes on his head. It had been easy for him to change his clothes; to change his house was going to be harder than he thought.

He glanced over at Rose who was apparently floating in the music. She was beautiful in her green silk dress and so self-assured. Was she really set against marriage? Perhaps she thought it absurd for old people to marry, but it was less absurd than living together and having to deal with May Dickens, Helen Abercrombie across the street and the neighbors on either side. Rose had been gone too long. She'd lived in France for too many years and forgotten how American middle-class morality swung its weight. The French could be terribly proper too, but she'd been exempt from their rules even if she had lived with a Frenchman.

I have been gone too long, thought Rose, as she watched the director's baton. Everything is still too strange to me. The orchestra is playing three times as loud as anything I heard in Paris, or is it this acoustically perfect auditorium? It's quite ugly. The French would have made it beautiful first and worried about the acoustics later. Oh, he's going to do *The Wedding March*. It will be horribly noisy. I wonder if it's still fashionable to thump it out on the organ at church weddings here? Everybody I knew used it when they married. I didn't. I wanted Purcell, Bach, Handel. Why is Theo sitting so rigidly? Has May Dickens frightened him? He needs loosening up. How good of George to act as if the whole incident was a farce.

The *Wedding March* rose over their heads and pounded in their ears. It was dreadfully loud, a weight to Theo, to Rose, merely a cliché.

CHAPTER FOUR

He simply couldn't hold off any longer. The urgency of early April, the new light green leaves, everyone's grass looking brighter—and full of weeds—the robins migrating north nearly all last month made him restless. The need to visit a nursery that morning and look at spring offerings absolutely possessed him. He hadn't gone to look at plants since Kate's death. The last two years he'd let his beds go; now they were almost bare except for the evergreens he'd planted as a background. If he really wanted a good price for the house, his agent suggested, a few blooming flowers would help. Graham Rivers was a bright fellow, had an optimistic outlook. Real estate had made him both rich and poor. He preferred to look on the sunny side. Theo knew effort was involved in adopting such a stance, however he saw Graham was not being professionally affable; he was naturally inclined that way. Certainly his ideas about selling matched Theo's abilities. Happily Graham hadn't mentioned the other old ploy, baking cookies to make a house seem homey. He couldn't imagine himself putting dabs of dough on a pan; he could see himself sticking bedding plants into loosened soil.

"Street appeal," Graham vowed, was always a good selling point. He wore a well-trimmed close beard, one despised by May Dickens who'd seen him walking up to Theo's door. She'd decided young people had too much hair these days.

"What about your father's day?" Theo asked. He led her off the track purposefully. If he told her his young bearded friend was an agent, she'd know he was selling the house. He meant to get that done without her interference. She'd question him every day if she knew, and more than that, she'd comment. Already he imagined her exclaiming, "You're not selling Kate's house surely!" He would become an item, a piece of May's collected news she'd carry to the grocery, the symphony, her church, to all the town.

"In my father's day?" May pondered. "That was then. Beards were worn mainly by older, well-settled, substantial men. Now they mean something different."

Theo shrugged. He couldn't get excited about the meaning of beards or long hair. If generations wanted markers, let them have them. May, he was sure, was only being opinionated as usual. She even talked back to news announcers on television when she disagreed with whatever they were saying. Stopping by two weeks after Kate's funeral to return an empty dish, he'd discovered this when he found May in her living room watching the evening news.

"I'll believe that when I see it," she said to a young man's face while he went on reciting his prepared script.

The announcer's voice continued blandly while May's objections ran on above, "For heaven's sake! What will you come up with next!"

Theo snatched his hand away from the doorbell, lowered the dish leaving it at the bottom of the screen, tiptoed across the porch and down the steps. Embarrassed for her over this private peculiarity, he'd tried to avoid speaking to May about the news from that day on. Even if they were next door neighbors, he soon realized that left them little to discuss although she persisted in telling him the bits of gossip she'd gleaned.

He put aside the catalogues he'd been idling through. Most of them came from nurseries in the north offering plants that would be overcome too soon by the unforgiving Texas sun. Rose's garden needed new plants too. They both had irises and old crepe myrtles that had survived. This year Ricardo's father Mr. Cantu who turned out to be a big, quiet man, had methodically pruned the crepe myrtles and oleanders at Rose's. They should fill out well. By July the crepe myrtle's watermelon colored pink blossoms would be dripping from their branches. And in the fall Mr. Cantu would divide Rose's irises the same way he did everything else, little by little, without wasting energy. Tall as he was, he worked deftly, never stepping on a plant or missing a weed. For him gardening meant patient tending. Theo wished he could be as patient himself, but now he really had to have something already blooming.

Having assured himself that he must go, Theo went out to his one car garage letting the back screen door bang. Forbidden to do so first by his mother, then Kate, and at last himself, he'd noticed lately he rather enjoyed being careless about a few things . . . strewing the newspaper through various rooms, letting magazines stack up, leaving glasses in the sink, habits he might have to correct when he lived at Rose's. In fact, since she inclined toward a slight disorder at her house, he might, on the other hand, cultivate a little more carelessness. Fortunately he'd already started clearing out the garage, so the major part of the job had been done. He'd sold the car about a year after Kate's death when it needed replacing. It was simpler to sell it. That was as far as he could think then. Hyde Park was in an older part of Austin where most everything he needed was in walking distance, and he liked to walk. He hadn't stranded himself.

Peering into the dimness while sniffing the familiar moldy earth floor, he located the boys' red wagon, the perfect carrier for bringing plants back from the nursery. He'd forgotten how silly he might look walking down the sidewalk pulling an empty red wagon behind him. There he was, mulling again over how he might look to other people. Didn't a person ever outgrow that? Other people really didn't care whether he pulled a red wagon down the street or not. It wasn't as if he were playing with one. He had an errand to do just as May Dickens and others did when they wheeled their empty carts back to the grocery store every week.

He and Max Ramsey, his neighbor across the street, used to do it together, get out their "little red wagons," Max called them, and parade over to O.T. Turner's nursery. O. T.—everybody called him Ott—had a little nursery, then married into the family next door, which allowed him enough acreage for a bigger one. He was the person responsible for all the exotic trees in

Hyde Park. People dug vast holes for catalpas because they liked the white orchid looking blooms in the spring, and because they were fond of their orange pods resembling miniature paper-lanterns in the fall, they bought Ott's trees of heaven. Now and then he sold a palm. Ott was gone now dead twenty years or more. Northers had killed most of the palms. A few remained—aberrant, steadfast reminders of people who believed they could grow anything if they only had enough water.

Max and Evelyn Ramsey were gone too, lost in a bad car wreck while driving to Houston to see their grandchildren. Someone else moved into their house three years ago. Theo hadn't bothered to find out who. Kate had been so sick then. All he knew was his new neighbors didn't garden much. Mowed and watered the grass every summer, but they seldom weeded or planted. Max had planted the few remaining narcissus and daffodils for his wife.

The wagon, rusty now, creaked as he pulled it out. Well, all right! He creaked too. He stopped just long enough to spray oil on the wheels, then out to the sidewalk he went, the wagon behind him, to find if those people who bought out Ott's descendants still carried bedding plants. What were Rose's favorites?

Homer, his leash attached to the handle of the wagon, gave him a mournful look as he padded along beside him.

"It's not dignified, but it's one way of getting a walk," Theo said. He couldn't cure himself of talking to the dog. He doubted he'd tried to very hard.

Just as he stared past her house, May Dickens appeared on her front porch, broom in hand, like a cuckoo popping out of a clock to announce the hour.

"Good morning, Theo," she called. Her head was all bundled up in a turban looking thing. At least she didn't seem to be balancing on loose springs today. He waved and walked on.

She came down the steps holding onto the broom still. "Come by on your way back. I've got some soup for you."

"That's kind, May. I'm not sure when I'll return though."

"Any time's all right. I'll be here."

Nearly every week she tried to inveigle him to come see her. She would be there and full of questions too. He did dread telling her he was selling the house. He'd made Graham promise to wait till the end of April to start showing it. Strangers coming up his walk would automatically start his neighbor jabbering.

He needed a few weeks to get plants started. Impatiens made a good show, the red ones especially, and they grew fast, but they were water guzzlers. Shasta daisies . . . zinnias, easy. Anyone could grow them. They would look good later. Now? Petunias, those old standbys, lavender petunias if they had them, dark purple and white if they didn't. Surely Rose would like those.

He stopped in the middle of the walk unintentionally jerking Homer's collar so hard it made the dog whimper.

"I'm sorry. I don't know what made me think Rose would like—"

Amazed at his presumption, he decided to call Rose from the nursery and ask if she wanted anything. He'd get pink . . . no, red for his yard . . . maybe both. Attention getters. Wheeling the wagon on toward the nursery he thought of the scent of petunias . . . sweet yet evanescent, their texture, a tissue-like crinkled softness spreading open in the sun.

He turned his attention to the sidewalk watching for buckling humps made by old tree roots until he looked up and recognized the Endicotts' house. Elisabet Ney had once come calling there and was refused entrance perhaps because she was wearing a jacket and trousers. Perhaps the Endicotts were only paying her back for not answering them when they knocked at her door during her working hours. She wouldn't permit social visits then. According to neighborhood tales, her telephone was wired to allow only out-going calls.

That afternoon on his knees next to Rose by her front flower bed where they were planting three dozen all white petunias, he told her about Ney's insistence on her own schedule.

"They called her eccentric, didn't they? I remember my parents talking about Elisabet Ney."

"Yes," Theo agreed. "Mine did too. She mystified everybody."

"I doubt anyone here had the least idea of the demands on an artist's life. Didn't most people believe they were simply odd, maybe crazy? Women artists were almost unheard of except for china painters and the occasional one who tried watercolors." Rose laughed. "Mother had a friend, Miss Louise Tevy, who copied postcards, mainly European landscapes, places she'd never been. She worked in oils, made smudgy little pictures of Venice's grand canal or the Swiss Alps. Everything was enlarged, but she never got the dimensions quite right. So sad, especially since the Impressionists were already well established in France."

"I imagine sculptors were almost unknown, even male ones . . . except those who carved tombstone figures. Ney's own father made his living that way. Well, it was the west," said Theo who was suddenly conscious of perhaps being thrown into the Philistine camp when compared to the French. "Most of those who settled Texas hadn't had enough time or education to acquire art appreciation."

"Humph!" Rose stood and stretched. "Melrose says some of them still haven't."

Theo smiled as he sifted dirt through his fingers. He liked the crumbly feel of it. Mr. Cantu had already added fertilizer and forked it in with what was there, years of accumulated unraked leaves, and lawn clippings, he supposed. The dark rich soil smelled of leaf mold, damp earth, promises, Theo might have said, though not to Rose. She had offered to come to his house and help him plant his petunias. He couldn't let her do that. Kate liked gardening. They had spent years together in their yard. Yes, he was selling their house, yes, he would move, yet contrary as he knew he was, he did not want to work there with anyone else. He would keep the memory of his wife in the garden they had shared. Let Rose believe what she might—that he didn't want to furnish conversation for May Dickens and the other neighbors, or he had a hard time letting people return favors, or he was being cranky.

Theo stood, brushed twigs off his trousers, and as he raised his head, heard a window being opened.

"Rose is that you? A woman's voice. "If it's not you, I'm going to call the police."

"Will she?" Theo turned to see Rose's face.

"Leila, of course it's me."

"I thought she was a recluse," Theo whispered.

Rose smiled as she heard the sound of the window being closed. "Oh, I thought so at first too, but I discovered she recently started a bakery. Her hours are so different we've had to no chance to meet until yesterday. She got home earlier than usual and came over to welcome me with a loaf of her fresh French bread. She's changed a recipe just a bit so she can use wheat grown in this country. Delicious."

She had missed French bread more than anything, missed stopping by the bakery for a fresh loaf nearly every day almost as much as she missed the taste of it, which was slightly different all over the country. Leila's tasted almost like the bread she and Thomas ate when they went down to St. Laurent la Vernede, a tiny place on the northwestern edge of Provence near Uzes, next to the Languedoc. He had a small house in St. Laurent where they stayed sometimes for a month in the summer or early fall. He'd adapted a remnant of the town's twelfth century wall; with the help of hired local masons and carpenters, rooms and three terraces were constructed on top of the wall. There were places to eat, to hang washing, to sleep, and to sun bathe. Although Thomas smiled at her wonder, Rose marveled over the age of the ancient stones. In the living room-dining area a huge fireplace like those in Normandy took up half of a wall, and above it was the loft where they slept. Next to it was a tiny kitchen, a bath, and hidden in the wall's foundation way below was an area holding the original well. Thomas covered the well with boards and divided the space into two rooms, one a cool extra bedroom, the other a wine cave. She liked going down to St. Laurent best in the fall when the grapes were being harvested. In the summer it could be so hot they had to sleep either in the earthy smelling cave bedroom or on a terrace. It reminded her too much of Texas then.

There was another place shared only with Thomas. She could not bring herself to tell Theo about it . . . about the narrow little secondary roads through the countryside, the vineyards lining them, the harvesters who returned to work there every year, the woods near Thomas's vintner's where a thirteenth century chapel had been discovered and lovingly restored. Thomas bought a case of red vin de Languedoc, and there was much talk about the quality of the grapes that year as well as how many years one should wait before opening the bottles just purchased. Afterward they went walking through the woods to find the plain looking little chapel . . . Norman, she thought, standing in a small cleared space in the sunshine waiting to be used by a family that no longer existed, open, therefore, to everyone who happened upon it. She couldn't see a way to recapture the yellow-gold-green colors of the trees, the crispness of the wind, or the perfection of that moment, and she hadn't the will to try.

There would always be those moments, those times past privately recalled, she was certain. She thought of the reserve she and Thomas had cultivated, all the memories of their first marriages they hadn't told each other. Neither of them were terribly secretive, but both of them knew, without discussing the matter, that parts of their lives could only be reclaimed individually. And more than that, she'd learned maintenance of this small distance was necessary; they had to leave each other room for private mysteries.

"Come on," she said to Theo. "That's enough for today. I'll get Mr. Cantu to take care of the others. I want to give you some of Leila's bread to try."

They went in talking desultorily about the problem of living alone and trying to consume whole loaves. Rose had never considered freezing half a loaf. Perhaps her feeling about the necessity of fresh bread was altogether French. Some prejudices, some tastes, apparently were acquired by living in a country. He didn't care. Rose could be as French or American as she pleased.

Later that afternoon, beginning to feel a little sore from unaccustomed bending and stooping, he planted half of his petunias. Deciding he might wait until the next day to finish the job, he started to rise only to feel a startling shock of pain in his lower back. He knew what caused it. He'd had it before. What was it called? One more he tried to rise, but the pain was so strong, radiating, probing up his back and down through his buttocks, he couldn't make himself stand upright. He waited panting a little, on his hands and knees by the flowers, then rolled over slowly as possible to his right side while pain pulsed up his spine. What was the wretched thing called? He lay on his right side imagining a spear stuck through one of the discs in his back, the soft tissues swollen, oozing through a narrow crevice made of living bone wrapped with nerves. Wanting to cry out, feeling it would be hopeless to try to take enough breath to do so, he lay on the damp ground breathing the smells of soil and new grass mixed with drifts of an orange-blossom-like scent blowing from the pittisporum bushes in full bloom.

He heard a mocking bird scolding a squirrel, probably sitting somewhere outside the bird's determined reach. No one knew where he was. Ted was far away in Mexico. Kenneth had left days ago. A wave of utter helplessness washed over him. He needed his bed, a hot pad, a painkiller, his young doctor's voice reminding him of what it was that had hit him.

The sun moved on, the lawn cooled, cars passed just by the other side of the red-tipped photenia he'd planted as a screen so many years before. It was so effective now no one could see him sprawled on the grass. Even the dog was inside probably standing by the door whimpering to get out. Well, Homer would just have to pee on the rug. How could he have allowed this foolish accident to happen? He'd known it could and denied it. Fully angry at himself, he groaned as he rolled back to his left side and tried to jerk his body upright. Once more, the pain stopped him. Defeated and still angry, he dozed off trying again to remember the name of his ailment.

Just before sunset he woke to see May Dickens, a pot of soup in hand, waiting on his front porch screeching his name.

For a moment he remained quiet. But who else could show up to call on him? Rose wasn't in the habit of dropping by. He wasn't supposed to see Graham until next weekend. The garbage men picked up on Friday, and this was Monday. At 5:30 in the morning, it would be too dark for the paper boy to see him.

"Over here." His voice quavered. She would call the emergency medical service. All right. Someone had to be called. Theo submitted to the result of his stubborn independence, the indignity of pain, and May Dicken's habitual curiosity.

In the confusion of giving directions and the chill creeping in after sunset, he forgot to ask her to tell the ambulance driver not to use the siren. He'd been laying there for hours already. What was the use of it other than the sheer pleasure so much clamor obviously gave the emergency crew? He heard them approaching blocks away, the siren moaning.

"Oh, damn!"

May blinked her eyes and pursed her mouth.

"Look under my bed and coax Homer out after I've gone . . . and watch for puddles."

"Can't I take him home with me? You don't know how long you'll be gone."

"I'm sorry about the puddles, May, but he's old and when he gets excited—" He feared he might make one himself before he got to the hospital.

"All right, Theo. It's all right. I had a dog myself once."

He allowed her to board Homer, allowed the emergency crew to slide him on a stretcher where he still lay sideways, allowed the nurse to stand by his bed while he swallowed pain pills the doctor ordered. After a drugged sleep, he had to let Doctor Wilkins hover over him early the next morning and make impertinent remarks about the continual need to do exercises for the lower back.

Finally Wilkins, a stocky fellow with dark brown eyes who appeared slightly inattentive at times, yet somehow saw everything, pronounced, "Spondilitis, inflammation of the vertebrae. Haven't you had it before?"

"Ah—"Theo was so relieved to hear the name of his trouble he forgot to tell Wilkins, as he usually did, that he could look it up on his record. Why else did doctors make notes? Instead he remarked on his age.

"Nothing to do with how old you are." Wilkins gazed just to Theo's right as though checking the position of his water glass. "Anybody can get this at any age. I've seen eighteen-year-olds with the same problem."

"Then I don't have to give up gardening?"

Wilkins shook his head. "Not if you do your exercises. And squat, don't bend from the waist."

"I was kneeling."Theo said.

Wilkins kept him in the hospital three days where he was visited by everyone including his real estate agent and Rose who promised she'd get Mr. Cantu to plant the last half of his petunias. Although he liked seeing them all, he was beginning to feel he'd be happy to get back to his accustomed solitude, an idea that worried him. How could he move to Rose's if he needed to be alone? However when he was alone once more, he began to realize he'd been subject to weakness imposed by simply staying in bed so long. According to Melrose, women had babies and got out of the hospital in only two days. Wilkins, heartless as usual, reminded him those women were less than half his age. Sometimes he wondered why he used Wilkins. A great diagnostician, he reminded himself, who had an office within walking distance. His friend Gerald used him too. He'd thought so well of Wilkins he'd meant to tell Rose about him.

As he grew stronger, his opinion of his doctor grew higher. Every morning, once the pain stopped, he carefully lowered himself to the carpet by his bed, hooked his toes on the rail holding the mattress, and while Homer lay beside him, his head on his paws, Theo did a short series of knee bent pull-ups followed by knee to chest crunches keeping his backbone flat against the floor.

"Don't be so disapproving!' He glared at the dog when he got to his feet. "Dr. Wilkins insists."

Homer yawned, rolled over, and stretched all four legs out stiffly as if in sympathy.

"That's better."

When Ted called from Mexico to check on him, Theo was feeling so much better he told his oldest son he believed he'd be safer living with someone. He and Kenneth need not worry about him any more. If he shared Rose's house, they could look after each other.

While Theo was in the hospital, Melrose kept telling Rose she should buy a car. She sighed unhappily at the prospect. Her granddaughter was determined to turn her into a true American again, one who lived on wheels and seldom walked anywhere. Her second reaction was driving would be dangerous; she hadn't driven in years. Melrose did what driving had to be done—taking the dry cleaning when there was any and delivering Rose to buy a week's worth of groceries, which took care of the bulk of the shopping. The store on Guadalupe was within walking distance. Rose, accustomed to neighborhood markets in Paris, happily walked over to pick up fresh fruit, vegetables, and any unforeseen needs. Melrose also drove them both to dentists, doctors, and the post office. Looking after the necessary mundanities was part of her life too.

During the early months of her return, Rose had allowed herself to believe when Melrose was gone she, like Theo, could depend on her own two legs plus an occasional cab. Now, if Melrose had her way, she would probably become one of those old ladies everyone hated being behind, one who drove around town too slowly and tended to be erratic about stop signs. Drivers following them, as Melrose sometimes had to, ran through a repertoire of curses while the ladies refused to take a chance on yellow lights.

Even after she'd recited these bleak possibilities Melrose continued to insist. "You wouldn't want to wait for a cab to take you to the hospital. Ambulances are sent only during emergencies. And it's too hot here to walk everywhere in the summer. I can't drive off to San Francisco and leave you here without any kind of transportation."

Leila advised her to give up. "You want to be our neighborhood anachronism? You can't. They gave me the title when I began making bread."

She couldn't ask Theo; his prejudices mirrored hers. He'd walked to the university the whole time he taught there and chided his students for causing parking problems.

"I know how to buy pictures, "she explained. "I love selecting jewelry. I know a bit about how to buy a horse, but I know nothing about buying cars. In fact," she threatened, "I may not remember how to drive. Don't you remember? Thomas did all the driving in France."

She was aware she was being unreasonable, but it occurred to her while her granddaughter was trying to get her to buy a car, she might get used to the convenience of driving, then before too many more years had passed, her son would be trying to get her to give up the car.

George promised to help. However nothing helped the appalling prices, and when she found out that a new car was worth at least five hundred dollars less the minute she signed the papers and drove off the lot, she refused to buy.

"Rose, it's something everybody knows and they all buy anyway." George stood beside her on 6th St. where ranks of Chevrolets gleamed in the lot behind them.

"I'll look for a used car."

He warned that decision had a downside too. She could

never be sure what she was getting. There were no warranties, no guarantees.

"I think I'd like a red one," Rose said. "Everyone should have a red car once in a lifetime. It's like having at least one red dress in your closet . . . or one solid red tie, don't you think?"

George grinned.

She would, she told the cheerful salesman who met them on the lot, test drive a red Chevy. Two years old, it had a radio, an air-conditioner, and a number of buttons which she had no intention of pushing, nor would she take time to listen to the salesman's flattering comments on what a fine choice she'd made.

When she drove the car off the lot, George commented, "See, your reflexes remember more than you thought they would." Then his quietly reassuring voice changed to a rasp. "Rose, you're going the wrong way. This is a one way street."

"I never noticed," she said. "They didn't have one way streets when I lived here before."

Amid irate honks, waves, and rude shouts, she turned down the first side street she saw and stopped. For a moment or so she sat there with her arms on the steering wheel gazing straight out the windshield at a stop sign on the next corner. Shocked by the knowledge she was extremely foolish and fortunate at the same time, she let go of the steering wheel, slumped down, and bowed her head.

"George, couldn't you—?"

"No you don't. You can do it, Rosie. It was just a mistake."

She turned toward him and asked indignantly, "What would you have said if I'd run into someone?"

"Come on, try once more."

After she'd quit shaking, she proceeded slowly around several blocks and returned to the dealer's. The young salesman, his short blonde hair emphasizing his sharp features, peered in Rose's window. A weasel, she thought. There's something weasel-like about him.

"I thought you were from Austin. I should have warned you about that one-way street."

Though he looked rather pale, he seemed genuinely apologetic and slightly uneasy also as if he were playing a part he didn't often play. Being startled doused all his cheer. Rose changed her mind. Not a weasel, a fox maybe, a startled fox.

"I am from here, but they have changed the streets around."

"Probably they have," he agreed.

Mollified by his sympathy, Rose added, "Of course I left Austin so long ago."

Despite George's final warning that a used car could have survived a wreck, and it could have been beautifully restored but still mounted on a bent frame, Rose decided she wanted the red Chevy. She hadn't paid any attention to the tape deck installed by a previous owner. However the salesman, regaining confidence, and perhaps too eager to justify an added expense, kept referring to it as "the newest customized eight-track stereo." Obviously he intended to tell her exactly how it worked.

"I can't understand why it's here," Rose interrupted. "Who wants more music in Austin? We've already got that marvelous classical station that plays all day long without any advertising."

The salesman glanced at George as if asking for help, but George kept his gaze fastened on the window where he seemed to be counting passing cars.

"Well . . . there are some people who. . . . I mean, you know. . . ."

Rose, uncertain whether she was being condescended to, or was being condescending, waited until she decided she didn't care. "I do know there are other kinds of music."

"Yes," the salesman said hastily and hurried on. "There's the problem of the signal fading out on the highway too. That station doesn't carry a long way. It's FM you know."

"I do. They tell you that all the time. I suppose this thing might be useful in case I ever leave town."

Following George in Melrose's car, she drove the red Chevy slowly home.

"Don't worry," Rose told him when they reached the house, "I intend to take lessons. I'll have to. There are probably a lot of new rules, and I've let my driver's license expire."

Melrose came out to admire the car parked in front of the house. When they were alone, George told her about the test drive.

"She did all right except for the one-way street, didn't she?" Melrose defended her grandmother.

George, walking through the yard behind her, lifted his eyes toward the sky. "The point is she could have had a wreck. I didn't know she didn't have a license. It was dumb of me, I guess. I thought she had an international-something-or other."

Melrose insisted that the point was Rose didn't have a wreck.

For the next few days Rose practiced parallel parking. Her reflexes seemed to have forgotten exactly how that was done. Belatedly, after bashing the front fender of Melrose's car, she remembered she'd never been careful enough about backing. Her tendency to reverse without checking appeared like a half-forgotten recurrent bad dream.

Melrose made a little sign—a pair of Os drawn as crossed eyes in large black letters warned LOOK BACK—and attached it below the rear view mirror.

To Rose her granddaughter's attention to her problem was more useful than the sign itself. Without quite knowing how it happened, slowly her driving improved until she was able to go over to see Theo after he got out of the hospital.

"Racy," he said when he first glimpsed the red car. The word slipped out before he thought. She affected him that way, he realized, startled him into unpremeditated announcements.

Rose laughed. "I thought you'd like it. Come on, Theo. I'll take you for a ride."

He waved in the general direction of May's house when they passed by.

CHAPTER FIVE

Theo was making up his bed in Melrose's old room. The task made him feel he was doing his part of the household work while Rose fixed breakfast. When he was through pulling the spread up he concluded he might be turning into a bit of an old woman in his age. He'd gotten particular about pillows. One looked lonely. He had to have two, and they had to be plumped fat every morning. He beat the pillows unmercifully and wondered who he was beating. Michael Hallaran probably. Yesterday he was in the front yard looking for the afternoon paper when the little boy called to him from his perch on top of the wall.

"Hey, you want your paper?"

Theo nodded.

"I got it." He held it out toward him. "The paperman threw it in our yard."

As Theo reached for the paper Michael asked, "Are you Mrs. Rose's daddy?"

With his head poked through the oleander bushes and the long green leaves framing his face, he had an innocent elfin look. Michael was only seven. Theo punched the pillow into shape. Children often got family relationships confused. His answer had been, "No, I'm too young to be her daddy."

"You're not too young to be my daddy." The child persisted.

"Yes, but you've got a daddy." Theo had taken his paper and retreated. By the next time they met Michael would have new interests, or he could think of some questions to ask him. When does your school begin? What's your favorite color? Do you have a middle name? Anything but family questions!

He went to the window. A few leaves were already falling. Too dry a summer and tardy August rains had never quite made up the loss. All the more reason to be thankful for live oaks. A tiny green hummingbird was beating his wings in front of the green acorns . . . nothing for him there. He'd better search the back garden. A delicious odor of fresh coffee came from the kitchen below. Rose bought the whole beans from a man who'd recently opened a store specializing in fresh roasted coffee. Each morning now she ground them. Her coffee was stronger than he was accustomed to; he'd learned to mix it half and half with hot milk as she did. Strange how he'd gotten used to so many new tastes—crepes for lunch, wine for supper—so many new ways of living this quickly.

It was his third month in her house. He'd sold or given away almost everything when he moved taking only one chair, his bed, a washstand that had been his grandfather's, a chest of drawers his mother left him, some bookshelves, and his books. He kept more of those than anything else; considering they furnished his mind, he felt more in need of them. He'd consulted Rose about her needs, but she declined all offers saying she had the necessities, so as planned originally, he sent everything else to his children.

Kenneth and Sally had surprised him by wanting some pieces; the old round oak dining table and chairs had been shipped to California. He wondered if their taste was changing from Scandinavian to Victorian. Perhaps they were just tired of a house full of spindly-legged teakwood. The brass bedsteads that Kate had bought, the dining room buffet, and all the mirrors went to Oklahoma for Ted and Margaret. They would get everything out of storage when they returned on vacation in December. The Mexican school year was reversed so that summer vacation fell during the northern winter. Every time he remembered this Theo considered the arbitrariness of time, the divisions various civilizations had made for themselves given the solstices, the equinoxes, sunrise and sunset. Gazing out the window still, his mind wandered from the mysteries of the Mayan calendar, the Egyptian one based on the solar system, the primitive sun dial—some archeologists believed—made by the enormous rocks of Stonehenge, the Julian calendar, the Gregorian, the Jewish, Mohammedan, Chinese, to each his own, a different calendar for each culture and sometimes one superimposed on the other. He never could get all the saints' days straight in Mexico. Could anyone? Weren't there correlations between them and the Aztec calendar's gods?

He couldn't remember how many times had he seen that calendar stone. Three or four, one for every visit he'd made to the museum in Mexico City. They had gone down there a lot when they were young. It was beautiful, cool in the summer, and comparatively cheap. But the last time he'd gone, it had begun to change. The city, always a place that attracted the poor, was beginning to be crowded with houses made of cardboard and tin, and the air was being fouled by fumes from cars and industries that insisted on locating in the capital. Built on an old lake bed, ringed by mountains, its mere location was damning. Like the Aztec calendar, reproduced a thousand ways—on cigarette lighters, belt buckles, women's brooches, paper placemats—the Mexico City he'd known when he was young was now overused, sadly corrupted. All the trees lining majestic boulevards had turned black and were dying. He mourned the loss of a city he'd loved; he didn't think he'd ever return to look on it again.

The pyramids just outside the city, how enigmatic, how severe, yet beautiful they were on that great plain. Regarding them through a haze of years—he had climbed the pyramid of the sun and waved to Kate on top of the pyramid of the moon—he thought of the strange distances between people. Kate, the one he'd been closest to was gone, he and Rose lived together though he seldom knew her mind. Rose had put an ocean between herself and Edward, and the same ocean between herself and the country of the man she'd loved; Melrose, by now, had flown half a continent away from George though she obviously loved him.

George was moving into the garage apartment later in September. He'd told Rose he'd like to take it the week before he left for California. Although finished building his houseboat, he'd decided it would soon be too cold. Too lonely, Theo amended. George, though a lot younger, was having a lot worse time of it than he was. When he returned he'd have to move and he'd also have to find an office, some place where he could set up a drawing board. He might even begin working at home in Rose's garage apartment. He hoped he'd have enough clients to make it necessary to go to a more businesslike address by the first of the year. Theo saw the risks he was taking; he also admitted to himself that he liked watching a young man take his chances. He'd taken so few himself moving from Cornell straight to Texas, just as he'd planned to, gone straight from one university to another, from one familiar set of hierarchies to another. George was ready to jump into wilder territory although he was staying in his own home town.

He went down to breakfast. Homer greeted him with a flop of his tail at the bottom of the stairs. When he moved to Rose's the dog, unaccustomed to a two story house, had tried to follow him up to his room which meant Theo had to carry him the last six steps, and Homer never had liked being carried. After the first few nights, contented that Theo would reappear in the morning, he'd found a place for himself by the first step. Rose had insisted the dog come with him, and Theo was grateful to her. He was used to Homer being around though he had been Kate's dog really, the only thing of hers he'd brought to Rose's house with him.

The first night he stayed downstairs by himself Homer prowled around growling at his own shadow on the floor. Theo had gone down to hush him and discovered Rose in her nightgown patting and soothing the dog.

"I thought we had a burglar," she said. Though her nightgown came down to her ankles, he could see the form of her body through the material swirling around her. He had a strong urge to go to her and checked himself. Overcome by elation and shock, he waited momentarily paralyzed.

"The moonlight . . . a new house," he stuttered not knowing whether he was apologizing for himself or the dog. "He'll quiet down. He's half deaf, you know. Hasn't any idea how much noise he makes. I'll take him upstairs if you like."

"No, it's all right. He's got to adjust sometime."

Without another word he fled to his room to stay awake for hours thinking about his predicament, happy he could still be aroused—he had supposed he could be by the right woman—frustrated because there was no honorable way to have Rose. He was well aware he was hopelessly old-fashioned; honor was perhaps too important to him, and more than honor, hiding behind its shield even, was the fear that Rose might not desire him. No matter how much these doubts tumbled in his head, the elation did not wear off.

Living in a state of exalted sexual tension, he could neither sleep nor eat well, yet he didn't mind. He took long walks by himself, told Rose she was a marvelous cook but he had a small appetite. On Saturday he roamed the museum so restlessly that Tim asked him, "Do you have some kind of trouble?" He admitted he did and refused to explain. If the flowering peach trees had not long ago lost their blooms, he would have broken off a branch of one in the park and carried it home to Rose. Lacking that he borrowed Rose's car and drove down to the corner of Lamar and 6th St. where he remembered a street vendor always waiting at that spot, getting lots of attention by juggling a carnation on one finger. Theo pulled in the parking lot behind him.

"Oh man!" the vendor said. "Man, I've been waiting for you!"

Theo, smiling to himself, bought every red carnation the fellow had in his bucket and carried them home quickly before they could wilt in the August heat.

On another day he gave Kate a single long-stemmed yellow rose and an inspired lecture on the Civil War origins of "The Yellow Rose of Texas." Just then her own garden, now beautifully cultivated by both Mr. Cantu and Theo, was full of flame-colored tea roses. These would not deter him. They already belonged to Rose. She must have his flowers, so he brought six stargazer lilies, and two days later, two dozen bachelor buttons and three dozen white daisies from the same florist who praised his choice of colors and threw in some greenery free. The living room began to look like an interior painted by Matisse. Obsessed as he was, he hardly noticed.

One night after supper later that week he pulled Rose's chair out, and while she stood beside it, he threw both arms around her.

In a frenzy of awkwardness he said, "It's the wine." They had drunk half a bottle. "I'm not used to it." He tried to look apologetic.

"Is it only the wine?" She smiled.

Fearful of understanding her smile, he blurted, "I . . . I don't know."

He backed away, and afraid of knocking something over, wheeled around and retreated to the living room where he began pacing the floor.

Stirred by Theo's activity, Homer began pacing with him. At the sound of the persistent click-click of the dog's nails on hardwood, he swooped him up in his arms, a difficult task as Homer wriggled wildly as usual and he'd gotten fatter. Now, apparently overcome by the sudden attention, he twisted about to lick Theo's face. Running to the front door, he dumped the animal outside and, feeling only slightly ashamed, made kicking motions toward him. Homer ran around to the side porch where he squeezed under the glider. Standing outside still, Theo wiped sweat and dog kisses off his face with his handkerchief. As he swung the door shut, its heavy brass knocker thudded behind him.

"Who is it?" Rose appeared carrying a tray holding coffee cups and a decanter.

He rushed to take the tray from her. "Just me. I was putting the dog out."

She sat on the sofa. His chair was a ludicrous distance away. He placed himself carefully—not too near, not too far—beside her.

"What's in that?" He pointed at the decanter.

"Cognac."

"*Madder music and stronger wine,*" he murmured. "Wonderful old Dawson. The part I always liked best was, *Flung roses, roses riotously.* You almost forget what he's complaining about. How did it go?" He held the decanter on his knee with one hand.

"Let's see." She leaned her head back and closed her eyes. "I can't remember it all but here's part, *I have forgot much, Cynara!*"

"*Gone with the wind.*" They both chanted. "*Flung roses, roses riotously with the throng.*"

"*Dancing,*" Rose's voice wavered. Then she went on by herself, her voice growing stronger as she recited,

Dancing, to put thy pale lost lilies out of mind;
But I was desolate and sick of an old passion,
Yea, all the time, because the dance was long:
I have been faithful to thee, Cynara! in my fashion.

"I memorized that my first year in college. Oh, such high-flown sentimentality!" She laughed.

"Do you think he did forget?" Theo asked.

"I used to think his *old passion* was an excuse for romantic despair, that he somehow enjoyed his misery."

"Oh." Theo liked the poem but was a little ashamed of his leanings toward high-flown sentimentality as well as romanticism.

"Actually, I like it. It's one of those shout it from the rooftop things." Rose took the decanter from him and poured a little brandy in both coffee cups.

"Would you— Do you suppose you would feel that way?" He put the cup and saucer down so it wouldn't rattle in his shaking hands. His heart was pounding crazily.

"Theo, if there's one thing I've learned it's this; I never know exactly how I'm going to feel about anything."

The strain was too great. Either he must leave the house and never come back or— He stretched toward her and kissed her.

"Rose, I—"

"I know, Theo." Taking his hand, she led him upstairs to her room where she undressed as if she were shaking off fetters. He fumbled his way anxiously out of his clothes. Thinking of the skinny depression below his own neck, his spare thighs, he had a moment's embarrassment he immediately forgot at the sight of Rose. Her body was more ample. Oh, how he had missed those curves of flesh, the full breasts, the spreading hips. She didn't wear a girdle. Funny. He thought all older women did. Kate had. Once in bed he quit making comparisons. There, in the long summer twilight, they made love for hours it seemed. They were both patient with each other, their hands and their bodies remembering lessons learned many years before. He knew he often seemed a timid man, but he was not timid in bed. Just as he rolled over on top of Rose, the dog began moaning to be let in. At the height of his pleasure, he no longer heard the dog.

For a long time after they lay talking peaceably, and since then they had slept together at least once every week, sometimes in her bed, sometimes in his. She seemed to catch a certain look in his eye or the touch of his hand on her arm. He never spoke of Kate, and she didn't mention Thomas.

As it turned out, both of them snored so, except when they made love, they kept to their own bedrooms. He was glad for two baths upstairs so they could avoid the elaborate moves around one sink which often reminded him of the mating dances of cranes. He could also avoid flossing his teeth in front of Rose, and she could hang her stockings to dry where she pleased. His old friend Gerald Dunham, who taught ancient history at the university, believed the finest of all of Rome's great engineering feats were running water and indoor plumbing. To those Theo added the fortunate possibility of separate bathrooms.

Rose called to him. I'm having breakfast on the porch. Come out."

"All right." He put his food on a tray and carried it outside. The wisteria, trimmed down from the trees and twined through the arbor again, was in its second lighter bloom, a miracle he'd worked with the help of Mr. Cantu. In November he would also help him dig up and divide the iris which, as Rose remembered, were all purple. Catching sight of a cluster of lavender wisteria and Rose wearing a blue smock sitting under it, he was sure he was the most fortunate old man alive.

"Do you want your mail now?" Rose asked.

"No, I'll look at it in a minute. You get anything interesting?"

While he ate she told him her news. She'd had a letter from Melrose in San Francisco. As usual she said very little except that George insisted on taking her on architectural tours to places she'd never heard of before. Phillip had written to ask if she'd found anybody else to live with them. And the postman reported that Helen Abercrombie had returned from Georgia. She planned to call on her that afternoon. Mr. Cantu and Ricardo would be working from nine till twelve, and she couldn't go off and leave them. Anne and Claus Tomlin were coming Saturday to take them out to dinner. There was a new movie in town she wanted to see. In the middle of telling him about the movie, she stopped.

He looked at her over his cup.

"Oh, Theo, I feel like a deranged idiot—all this scurrying around, making plans. I was going to come back here, dig in my own garden, and be happy in my old age!" She threw her hands up and let them fall to her lap. "Sometimes I feel we might as well live in one of those retirement villages and have planned activities, group outings—"

He raised his hand. "I'd rather die first, and so would you. Here you can pick and choose among the generations, see young and old friends, live exactly as you like. You have a gift for attracting all sorts of people. Why do you deplore it?"

"I don't, but why must I rush around so? I have this terrible restlessness."

"Did you expect to sit in a corner with your hands folded?"

Rose laughed. "No. I didn't expect I would be quite so active though. Some days I think. . . ."

He waited silently. She usually left her sentences suspended when she thought she was going to say something unpleasant.

"I think I'm simply trying to busy myself, to flee, to run away from death."

The hummingbird had discovered that the wild trumpet vine trying to work its way through the wisteria had a few late August blooms. He watched it whirring above them, the dark green body with wings beating much faster than his own heart. The intensity of the bird's search for food balanced against its short life span, how hard it worked. Endeavor only equaled futility. And for man? Well, there was something more—a longer span if one was fortunate and much more of course, yet in her present state of mind, he didn't think he'd better list the joys of life. He turned his eyes back to Rose. "Perhaps you are only very much alive."

"Or terribly afraid." She shrugged her shoulders as if to shake off a mood, laid her breakfast tray aside, and crossed her legs. "Look what I found yesterday." She drew a pack of cigarettes out of her pocket.

"I didn't know you smoked."

"I don't. These are Galoiuses . . . the smell of them! Like France. They sell them at the student bookstore on Guadalupe. I'm going to try one." Holding the cigarette in the middle of her lips, she lit it with a kitchen match. Smoke puffed out the sides of her mouth.

"Oh! It tastes awful."

She leaned down and dropped it in an ashtray. An acrid sweet smell blew toward him.

When she straightened up big tears rolled down her cheeks. At first he thought the cigarette had caused them, but as the smoke cleared to a wavering line he saw the tears were falling still.

"Rose, what is it?" He'd never seen her cry before. She sat upright crying silently, tears running unchecked, like the statue of a female saint he'd seen in Mexico, a Maria Dolorosa who was said to cry miraculously once every year.

"Nostalgia. Something. I don't know. I haven't cried in a long time." She jumped up and ran in the house. Uncertain about following her, Theo waited a few minutes, heard her go upstairs and slam the door. No, he wasn't wanted. He couldn't tell her not to cry when she probably had good reasons for crying. Women always seemed to have sufficient reasons for tears. When she finished they would talk.

The front gate creaked. Too early for anybody else, must be Mr. Cantu and Ricardo. He listened to the footsteps coming up the stone stairs and across the terrace.

"Buenos días, Señor Isaac."

"Buenos días, Ricardo."

He knew a little Spanish. Everybody in the state knew a little. For fear of giving offense or stumbling into saying something laughable, he'd remained silent. Only lately had he allowed himself to practice the language. He might mispronounce a word or use the wrong one, and Ricardo wouldn't correct him although he'd asked him to.

Kate advised him to keep trying and keep asking. The French, she'd told him, had never given up correcting her.

He and Ricardo stuck to greetings usually.

"My father has asthma. He becomes sick with so much rain. He is unhappy he cannot come. You tell Mrs. Rose I do the work today, please? My father will come next week. I go to school then."

"You must go sometime."

"It will be better this year maybe."

"Good. You want to read the paper to me now?"

"You tell Mrs. Rose first, please."

Theo went upstairs and after waiting for a moment outside, knocked on Rose's door. Her eyes were dry. The tears had been smoothed and powdered away. "It's Ricardo. His father is ill. He says he'll work today. I want him to read for me first. It's his last lesson before school starts."

"I'd forgotten the schools opened so early. Monday is Labor Day, isn't it?

Theo nodded.

"You know what we should do?" Her face brightened. "We should give that child a holiday."

"Yes," he agreed, "but how?" He did not want to simply pay Ricardo for a day's work and let him go. That would be generous, but he admitted, he wanted the boy around. He looked forward to him coming each Thursday.

"You go on down and give him his lesson. I'll make a picnic lunch. We'll take him to Barton Springs."

"Perhaps he doesn't know how to swim."

"Oh, never mind! There's plenty to do out there. He can wade, and there's a playground and the train. Go on now. I'm coming." She smiled gleefully. "We can all ride the train."

Ricardo did know how to swim. They watched him from the bank while he dived into the clear cold water. Both of them, still fully clothed, sat in the shade of a big pecan tree until Rose gave way to languor and stretched out on the quilt she'd brought. The height of the tree growing in what used to be bottom land overlooking Barton Creek made her think of the tall chestnuts in the Bois de Boulogne. Strolling under them on a trail with Thomas, she noticed, just as Melrose did later, the elegant horseback riders.

"English style riding is so different. I grew up with quarter horses and heavy western saddles covered with all that tooled leather. Thoroughbreds are much taller and lighter looking . . . skinny aristocrats compared to our chunky peasants."

Thomas laughed at her description. "You make our horses sound effete."

"I expect they would look that way to many westerners."

A few days later she'd discovered him early in the morning standing beside the bed fully dressed in riding clothes.

"My Lord! I . . . I thought for a minute I was dreaming about living in the nineteenth century."

"Madame." He bowed and handed her the pair of cowboy boots she'd had mailed from home. He'd borrowed two horses to take her riding in the Bois.

They were taller than any horses she'd ever ridden, the saddles, mere trifles of leather, the stirrups beneath them, thin pieces of metal dangling from narrow straps.

"Thomas, I don't know how to ride a . . . a French horse."

He laughed and mounted, "Like this. It is not hard. A horse is a horse."

She gathered up the reins, confused because there were four instead of two, and tried to climb on without knowing quite where to put her hands since there was no horn.

"You do not cling to the saddle horn do you? The cowboys I watch in your movies never seem to."

"No, but how do you get up? There's nothing to grab hold of."

He dismounted, came over and placed her hands on the saddle properly.

As soon as she was on the horse's back she gripped the saddle between her knees.

"Let go. Put your feet, the front part of them, in the stirrups. A Texas woman!" He teased gently while showing her how to weave the reins through her fingers and to balance herself on the balls of her feet in the stirrups. Her legs trembled, and she willed herself to control her quivering muscles fearing if she communicated her uncertainty to the horse it would bolt. Thomas trotted off in front of her. She followed at a slow walk. He posted effortlessly keeping his back straight matching the rise and fall of hooves. The wide trail was covered by arcing branches. Concentrating on keeping in the saddle, she was barely conscious of being in a forest. Her reins slipped out of her grasp. She bent forward holding onto the horse's mane until she caught up with Thomas who had stopped at a crossing. Just as her horse walked up beside his, a young woman dressed in a dark brown riding habit cantered in front of them and disappeared. A man followed her riding fast and shouting her name in a pleading voice, "Amelia!" Rose looked down at her slack reins, her faded blue jeans, the scuffed pointed tips of her cowboy boots showing under them, and vowed she would one day look like Amelia dashing through a glade with Thomas riding after her. She bought her own riding clothes—the proper boots, jodhpurs, jacket and velvet covered hard cap.

"For safety, Madame," said the clerk who, like most French clerks walked the thin line between being deferential and critical. That clerk had probably never been on any kind of horse's back in her life, but she was certain about how a rider should look.

Later Rose took lessons, "to go with the horse and the clothes," she said. Actually she was delighted to be out-of-doors more often.

Sighing, stretching a bit, she stared up though the pecan tree's branches to slices of sky.

Theo, at first, had been startled when she lay back; soon after he stopped feeling embarrassed. There were a lot of older people out that morning, many of them lying about on rocks exposing their leathery skins. He'd already taken off his coat and tie, but he couldn't give up his shoes and socks even though he felt he still had on too many clothes. He pushed his toes back and forth in his shoes.

"We should have brought our bathing suits," Rose said lazily.

"I haven't got one." Theo stared at his shoelaces. "And I'm afraid of looking ridiculous."

Rose nodded toward the group on the rocks opposite. "We couldn't look any worse than any of them."

He thought about it, tried to see himself among them, one more old sea turtle lumbering to the beach to sun. He wondered if he could climb the rocks without falling. They didn't seem difficult. Perhaps it would be better to do it all at once, walk out almost nude wearing nothing but a bathing suit. Taking his clothes off bit by bit was agonizing.

"I will go and rent a suit if you will," she dared him.

"They will look terrible."

"Probably, but I can't stand to sit here all dressed and look at that water one minute longer. I think it's hotter now than it was the first of August."

"All right. I'll do it."

Ricardo gave a whoop as he jumped off the high diving board. Theo waved toward the bathhouse when he surfaced. Ricardo nodded. He was waiting for them when they came out. He was sure the boy's natural politeness kept him from remarking on their appearance. He and Rose both laughed when they saw each other dressed in suits of identical light green stuff that resembled wool. Rose's suit sagged in front, and his drooped over his thin flanks. They walked sedately down a long flight of steps, Ricardo in the middle, and without discussing where to get in, went together toward the shallow end.

"It's cold," Ricardo warned.

"I know. I remember," Theo said, but he'd forgotten how cold. Rose watched him dubiously then chanted, "One, two, three." They ducked themselves up to their shoulders. The cold was shocking. It could kill him, would if he didn't move.

"Come on." Ricardo called. He was halfway to the rocks.

He began swimming, thrashing his legs vigorously. Rose was behind, he thought. Opening his eyes he looked at the rocky bottom, blue-green, darker blue-black, sun falling in ripples. A tiny perch flashed out of a crevice. He raised his head to breathe and turned over to float, near death, nearer to life still. The sky seemed almost turquoise colored. He paddled his feet. How could anyone swim the length? They must practice all summer. He shivered as he crawled up on the rocks. Rose was swimming beautifully, regularly, four strokes, turning her head for air on the fourth. He would lie down in the sun and wait for her.

"Theo," she gasped as she flopped down beside him, "we both forgot and we ought to know better. Both of us. We've been swimming in this pool since we were children. This is the coldest part. The springs bubble up right down there."

Ricardo suggested they walk around the pool instead of swimming back. Theo looked at the rocky bank and said he'd rather swim. He tried to see if there was anyone he knew on the ledge above but could not distinguish faces.

Rose decided she wanted to swim back also. First, though, they must sunbathe. Ricardo warned them about sunburn then left to clamber across the rocks to the diving board.

They both lay silent, dreaming, Rose of a beach in Brittany where she and Thomas had been the preceding August, Theo of the long summer days of his youth when he'd learned to swim in the river, the dark Colorado that wound through the surrounding hills. The air was light and sweetened by the smell of freshly mowed grass. He could have gone to sleep except for the rock.

Lunch took a long time. Theo and Rose napped side by side while Ricardo explored the playground. When they awoke it was nearly three.

"The train. We must ride the train," said Rose. "Wouldn't you like to, Ricardo?"

"If you like to." He would not ask for anything.

Theo bent down to him. "Say yes, so Mrs. Rose can ride."

"All right. Yes."

Rose bought him a big sack of popcorn right before they all got on the miniature train. The engineer was a man about his own age, Theo guessed, wearing all the proper gear; striped overalls, a yellow shirt, a red bandanna, and a peaked cap. Behind him they sat erect like two proud grandparents taking their grandson on an afternoon excursion. The tracks went by the playground, the lower half of the pool, the creek, the lake. They were carried halfway around the park and back again; the train moved slowly through a deep green haze, the last confident burst of summer that would not really end until November northers stripped the trees.

CHAPTER SIX

Theo walked across the University of Texas campus to meet Gerald Dunham at his office. They would talk about the department, who had been promoted, who hadn't, who was leaving, who had been hired. Gerald, ten years younger and still teaching, was his best contact. Though Gerald had come to see him when Kate died and had called him many times afterward, Theo, chained by paralysis of will, hadn't been able to set foot on campus. He hadn't been inside of Garrison Hall since he retired. He didn't like feeling he was an outsider, a professor emeritus pressing his nose against the academic window. Since he started coming over to the campus for concerts with Rose, however, he felt less ill at ease.

After all, it was his university. He'd gone to undergraduate school when there was nothing more to it than a collection of wooden shacks scattered around one large brick building. And now, the place was monstrous . . . monstrous, he repeated to himself. A new women's dormitory that resembled a luxury hotel five stories high covered the ground where Victorian houses had stood, and they were in the middle of construction everywhere else, sopping up intramural fields, crowding into all the open spaces. Old buildings were torn down, new ones erected although there were still a few World War 11 surplus barracks still being used as classrooms on the fringes of the campus. He obliterated them all trying to begin again, to remember how the place had taken shape, a restoration interrupted by a group of young women chattering as they swirled by. They seemed to be dressed in some kind of costume, bright colored stocking and terribly short dresses. Perhaps they were drama students, pageboys, on their way to a dress rehearsal for the annual Shakespearean performance. No, it was too early in the year for that. Another solitary young woman on the sidewalk opposite was dressed in the same way. A fad . . . well, he was certainly slow to catch on. Legs, the women seemed to be all legs, flamingos of all colors, yellow, green, red, bright blue, pink, black, lots of black. What did his colleagues do when they had to face a room full of vari-colored knees? Did they shuffle their notes and address themselves to the nearest set of questioning eyes? After all, they were historians, men practiced in methods of observing, recording, accepting. Skirts short, affluence; skirts long, depression. He wasn't sure it held true, but it was comforting to have a theory to fall back on. Once within the campus boundaries, he found it all too easy to fall into academic patterns of thought, to categorize colored stocking as Elizabethan and short skirts as economic indicators. Pigeonhole what is new and it's no longer strange or even frivolous but only repetitious.

The Tower clock began to ring the hour. Theo looked at it with disgust. He should have gotten used to the Tower by now. It had been standing there since 1936. At one time he had begun to see it as only another example of a strange mixture of architectural fantasies. There were two L-shaped wings full of offices, atop these Italian gardens grew, and in the middle a tower shaft rose twenty-seven stories high crowned with a copy of a Greek temple where the carillon's bells hung. A viewing ramp, horribly attractive to suicides, circled its crenellated base. The whole tower was bathed in orange light any time the football team won a game. When a mad student used its ramp for an outpost and murdered sixteen people in a few hours, Theo ceased regarding the Tower as a familiar sore thumb sticking in the sky. It was ugly. It would be ugly until the day he died. Students poured out of surrounding classrooms to fill the huge paved square in front. Did they remember the day it had been clear except for fallen bodies? Or had they forgotten already? Except for the older ones, he expected the last was true. The French went on living in Verdun, the Germans in Berlin, the Japanese in Hiroshima. The Vietnamese hadn't given up living in Saigon. The living walked across the sites of catastrophes every day. It was natural, wasn't it? Ah . . . the trouble with the long view was it led to complacency . . . or it could. At times he thought that all a history teacher did was to give excuses, precedents for future bloodshed.

Entering Garrison's dark hall, he noticed how crowded it was and nearly bumped into one of the younger professors who recognized him but didn't remember he'd retired.

"Oh, yes," Theo assured him. "Five years ago. Time to get some more new men in."

There was no use repeating himself to Gerald. They had argued the point many times before. Older teachers had so much experience, he always said, while Theo wanted to make sure of room for younger ones who might have different ways of thinking about the past. "History changes," he would say, "according to the historian." That always ruffled Gerald who taught ancient history and was proud of the parallels he could find in the modern world.

When Theo arrived at his office, he found his former colleague sitting behind his desk, his feet resting on an open drawer, Gerald rose to shake hands.

"You haven't changed, Theo. I wish you were still teaching."

"Humph! I used to think students were at least eighteen. They all look about twelve-years-old to me today."

"You'd like the students. You always liked them, but I will say these are different from the kids we taught earlier. When they're not protesting, they're studying so they can avoid the draft."

"I can't blame them, Gerald. Vietnam is a horror. Remember old MacArthur's advice, 'Never get involved in a land war in Asia.' We should have taken it long before now." He lowered his voice. "I've spent some time trying to track down how we got into it, and I'm still baffled."

He smiled as he looked down. Gerald still wore voluminous trousers that fell in soft folds on top of his shoes. People's habits were strangely reassuring.

"Theo, at least three or four students, out of every twenty

of mine, are militant pacifists. And that isn't a contradiction of terms. Many of them would embrace your favorite idea of the guilty historian. Trouble is, they would also write it on a banner over the front door of Garrison, then go out and start a protest."

Theo shook his head and said he doubted that his course in the American Revolution would be particularly popular or helpful.

Gerald laughed. He busied himself with his pipe for a moment, knocking it into an already overflowing ashtray and Theo, familiar with his delaying tactics, knew he was getting ready to propose something.

"There are too many of them for us, Theo. We've had to add eight new men this semester and the teaching assistants for the freshman courses— There are so many of them they have to share corners of desks. Have you ever . . . would you consider teaching again? Even one course would be a great help."

He studied his friend's face. Was it kindness that prompted the offer? Was the department that desperate?

"I'm an old man."

"So am I. Neither one of us is tottering. I've never heard you complain of your health."

"I have a check-up once a year, and so far, other than a little back trouble and the kind of arthritis everybody gets when they get older, I've been lucky. I'd say it's because I don't smoke and do walk a lot, but that's nonsense. We've both known of men a hundred-years-old who attributed their longevity to a pint of whisky and a good cigar every day. Old age is a curse even with good health if you don't have some way to keep busy. Do you know what I do with my time? I read a lot still. I go to more movies than I've ever gone to in my life, and to concerts, to art shows sometimes. I watch the war news most nights, though sometimes it's so awful I turn it off. I'm a living room war coward. On Saturdays I keep the Elisabet Ney open, and on Thursday afternoons after he gets out of school, I tutor a young boy."

"History?"

"Mostly English. He needs more help with it than anything else. I throw in a little history when I can. He's an interesting child, curious about everything. I'd forgotten how curious a young boy can be." He went on talking about Ricardo, thinking, I should tell him about Rose. Why can't I be as open as she is? She told me right away she'd lived with Thomas all those years in Paris, didn't marry him though. Why not? Would she marry me for the sake of convenience? I can't tell Gerald I'm sharing a house with Rose Davis, and I certainly can't tell him we're sharing beds . . . as if there was any need to. Shocked by the bragging adolescent hidden in his mind, he fell silent.

"I'm afraid of my own retirement, Theo. I think I'll teach till they send me home in a wheelchair. I don't know how to do anything else. And I refuse to take up something like making pots or weaving rugs. My God! Half the older men I know are learning how to make lop-sided bowls. I won't do it! I never was any good at making things, not even model airplanes." He tamped the tobacco down in his pipe with his thumb. "I may move to Italy when I have to retire. Might as well live with the Italians. I've been teaching Roman history all my life." He lit his pipe and leaned back. "You think that's ridiculous! I can see—"

"No, I was thinking about all the people who came to Texas country in search of some sort of utopia, people like Elisabet Ney and George Montgomery. They landed in Georgia with ideas about founding a more perfect democratic community. All they found was malaria. So they moved on to Texas, tried to farm at Liendo, and got poorer every year. Her studio in Austin was probably the nearest thing to a utopia she ever had. As for him, the time he had for experiments, time to think and to write was, I expect, his greatest freedom."

Gerald waved his hand in deprecation. "I don't expect to find one anywhere, and it's too late now to make one. I've spent years teaching ancient history, and I've learned, like Yeats, though for different reasons, naturally, that *This is no country for old men.* I want an old place, old customs, old steps, old stones."

"I have a friend who lived for many years in France. She says she became more American there, was more conscious of being an American, than she was when she lived in the states."

"Yes, I expect so. I don't want to escape my nationality. After a year or so in Italy I may come running back with my tail between my legs. I've lived there before though, in Sienna, and I liked it. I can speak Italian. So can Louise. She wants you to come to dinner with us. Saturday night?"

"All right. Could I bring someone?"

"Fine. Anyone we know?"

Theo swallowed. "It's a friend, Rose Davis."

"Good . . . good for you. It's time you had somebody."

Gerald relaxed into benevolence easily. Though he would try to console people in a crisis, he really preferred to believe his friends were happy.

"She's the one I spoke of, the one who's lived in France."

"Ah, well, we'll look forward to talking to her." He stood up to shake hands. "What about the job, Theo? Will you help us out?"

"I'll let you know Saturday if that's all right."

The bell announcing the end of the hour clanged in the hall. Theo, hearing the familiar sound, decided he was glad he no longer had to listen to every hour being rung away. He should have told Gerald then. No, it could wait. Time was his, not the bell's.

Leaving Gerald's office he joined a crowd of students outside. One thing was certain; he must ask Rose to marry him. She would have to be persuaded. How had he proposed to Kate? Did he ever actually say, "Will you marry me?" Strange not to be able to remember such an important question. He must have asked her at some point, yet when he tried to remember all he could recall was a moment of mutual accord. Then he'd gone to ask her father's permission, a little worried but willing to go to him and say he would have his degree from Cornell that spring and a job waiting for him in Texas in the fall. He could take care of Kate. He was that young, thinking all he needed to take care of a wife was a job and a declaration of love. Kate's father had been kind to him, surprised him by offering whisky at three; usually nothing but tea was served before four. Time was exactly meted out in that household, so much for this, so much for that. He was granted a one hour interview alone with old Mr. Meyers in his library. The bottle of rye and two shot glasses were kept in a locked desk drawer. A coal fire was burning. The room was well lit; four long windows with discreet glass curtains filtered gray-white northern sun. They sat in wing chairs on either side of the fireplace drinking whisky neat. The back of the chair was higher than his head. It made him feel uncomfortably small. Rye burned his throat as it went down. It was the only time in his life he drank whisky without ice.

"Texas," Mr. Meyers pronounced the name of the state carefully as though it were a foreign country, "is a long way away. How can I let you take Kate so far away from her home? We would never see her again. I approve of you personally, but I do not approve of you vanishing to the west with my daughter. Can't you get a position somewhat nearer?"

Fully aware of Mr. Meyers's prejudices, Theo had his argument prepared. "I've already accepted this one, sir. I was born in Austin, and I've always planned to return. It wouldn't do to go back on my word. We might arrange to meet at least once a year at a halfway point, Cincinnati, perhaps." Cincinnati was certainly more than halfway from Austin to Ithaca, but he and Kate were young. They could stand the journey better, and until they had children, he could not imagine Mr. Meyers would be willing to go farther south. His family, originally from Germany, had settled mainly in New York state. Theo had told him about German pioneers in Texas, towns near Austin called Fredericksburg and New Braunfels, but the westward movement had never appealed to Kate's father. Fortunately he had a younger brother living in Cincinnati. They agreed to meet there every year. Old Mr. Meyers snapped the cover of his pocket watch shut when the hour was over. Old Mr. Meyers. Why had he seemed so old? Because he was so much the

German patriarch? He couldn't have been over fifty-five. Wasn't it all a matter of where one stood, twenty-five and looking up to fifty-five, or seventy looking back on it?

Theo smiled to himself as he continued across the campus thinking of Kate as she was in the twenties. Her father wouldn't let her bob her hair. She'd shortened her skirts, lifting them inch by inch so as not to astonish him. The strategy worked. By the time they were married Kate's skirts had risen to just below her knees. She had taken great delight in raising them just above her knees after they married. Her nightgowns, though, had been floor length like the one Rose had on the night the dog barked so much.

He took the slow way home through the middle of the campus past the women's gymnasium and past the kindergarten run by the university. Michael Hallaran's little sister Megan was out on the playground sitting in a swing. He waved. She didn't seem to see him. Did Rose see him? Was he anything to her other than a lonely old man? They were companions weren't they? What did she have against marriage? Ridiculous to be so old and have young problems!

Rose slammed the front door behind her so hard the knocker rattled like shot splattering against wood. She'd finally gone across the street to see Helen Abercrombie who turned out to be a weedy looking old woman—a stalky dandelion among the zinnias. Rose remembered her being fashionably slender when she was younger. Now in her house everything was over-stuffed except the owner. She sat in a fat pink velvet chair, wooden roses curling in an undeserved garland behind her head, gave her visitor bad coffee, and passed her particular brand of melancholia along with stale cake.

Rose went into the downstairs bathroom to brush her teeth. Toothpaste tasted infinitely better than Helen's coffee and cake. If only Theo were here! Should Helen ever return the visit she must be sure he was home. Most of her questions had been about him. Rose turned back to her living room feeling slightly relieved at the sight of her own disorder. The place was getting cluttered. No matter where she lived she accumulated a magpie's nest—books they were both reading, a stack of Sunday editions of the *Times*, Michael Hallaran's recorder he'd left on top of the piano, Melrose's pictures covering the walls, piles of sheet music, Theo's old Morris chair he'd brought with him. She sat down in it putting her arms on the chair's. Beneath them were fierce lions' heads complete with carved wooden teeth. Rose curled her fingers around the teeth. Helen Abercrombie reminded her of the first concierge she'd had to deal with, the old woman at her apartment house in Paris. Madame Duchard had *la grippe* half the year, or so it seemed; Helen complained of perpetual hay fever. They both had a sad outlook, and they expressed it in the same way—first, moan over all their own family's problems, then inquire mournfully about their listener's misfortunes. One was supposed to join them in a dirge that led eventually to a world-wide catastrophe and universal doom. Madame Duchard could progress from a bad cold, to her daughter's wretched housekeeping, to a general condemnation of youth, skip to the wickedness of the ungodly Communists, and from there it was only a short step to atomic holocaust.

Rose stroked the lions' curly manes. Theo had warned her that Helen was full of depressing tales, yet she was determined to be on speaking terms with her neighbors. Helen and she had been in some of the same organizations when they were both young married women. She went to see her depending on her own methods of dealing with whiners, to listen, to sympathize, and finally to make them laugh. Even Madame Duchard would laugh over the ridiculous price of a pair of stockings or an argument with the butcher; Helen could not be drawn past her insatiable desire to complain. Evidently bleakness gnawed at her, so she loosed it on anyone within speaking distance.

"My daughter had to have a complete hysterectomy this summer. You know, I suppose, that Kate Isaac died of cancer?" Helen sputtered out before she finished pouring coffee.

Rose nodded. She suffered from arthritis, bad feet, and terrible teeth yet considered these merely the indignities of age combined with genetic mischance when such ailments were compared to major surgery, heart trouble, or cancer. Still she was tempted to groan about her ingrown toenails if only to steer Helen away from the subject of Theo. Instead she waited—half repelled, half fascinated—to hear how Helen would wriggle back to her point.

"Cancer seems to kill so many people nowadays. It isn't supposed to be catching, but I sterilized all the dishes at my daughter's house this summer—burned my hands doing it too. All that extra work. It was bad for my heart, I'm sure. How's Theo's heart?"

"It's in excellent condition as far as I know. Do you do any volunteer work now, Helen? You used to be so active in the hospital auxiliary."

"Other than looking after my daughter, no. I've gotten too old. It takes me the rest of the year to recover from a summer in Georgia. Have you recovered from the summer here yet? With Theo there you must have a lot more work to do. Men always require so much attention."

"Oh, I'm lucky I guess. The garden is pleasant. Theo likes working out there early in the mornings. He's good about training vines. We've gotten the fountains started again. A lot of water sprayed about gives an illusion of coolness." She'd managed to escape that barb. How would Helen contrive another?

"You should be careful about bending and stooping in the heat. I hope Theo hasn't been working too hard in the yard. A lot of exercise for a man his age is dangerous. Isn't it terrible the way so many of our presidents have had heart trouble! We ought not to put sick men in the White House. How can men who are having heart attacks all the time make the proper decisions! Just look how long this war has dragged on. Oh, we could use the bomb, but I guess that would be just as bad for us, wouldn't it?"

"I have a fine yardman. He's done miracles," said Rose defiantly refusing to comment on military strategy. She continued, "Even living across the street, you can't imagine how overgrown the place was. And the things we found! Any number of bottles in the hedges!"

"Probably all on Miss Leila Howard's side of your house. Her father used to drink so much. He took up sherry when she hid the whisky, and that made things worse since it's stronger, you know. He died early. He was only fifty-seven. Of course after all these years in France you must be accustomed to the effects of alcoholism. My husband— You remember John? Well, as everybody in town knows, like Leila's father, he drank himself to death. I never had any use for the stuff. The French us it a lot in their sauces, don't they? Their children must be reeling in the streets."

"When wine is heated the alcohol evaporates I believe. I have never been sauced!" Rose gave her a wry glance.

Helen shifted her spindly legs showing an edge of petticoat but not a glimmer of a smile.

"I must go," said Rose with more force than she intended.

At the door Helen warned her, "Be careful crossing the street. People are always getting run down in front of their own houses. A truck driver murdered my brother-in-law in Houston last year. Theo gave up his car didn't he?"

"Sometimes he drives mine. Actually he prefers to walk." Rose dashed down the steps to her own house. She doubted she'd see her again unless Helen's obviously latent social conscience forced her to repay the call, or more likely, her gloominess pushed her to it. At least Helen lived across the street. In Paris she'd had to see Madame Duchard every day.

At first she was sure she'd never get used to the woman. There was nothing Madame Duchard could do for her except to leave her alone, the one service she wouldn't perform. Every time Rose came in or went out she was conscious of being watched though all she might see was a bit of Madame's black skirt or hear her raucous croak, "Bonjour, Madame Davis." The greeting was almost enough to ruin a day. Before she left the Rue de l'Abbeye, she was quite used to Madame D. and would have missed her if she hadn't been there. She was part of the house like the door forever creaking on its hinges. She'd made her peace with Madame Duchard by having a granddaughter. During the beginning weeks in Paris while she was still living in a halfway state between being a tourist and a settled person, Rose had wandered about the streets a lot. There was nothing she needed for herself except food, so she shopped for Melrose buying lovely, impractical little girl's clothes and a collection of French dolls in regional costumes. Madame Duchard caught her coming in with her packages and told her where she could mail them. Rose confessed to spoiling a four-year-old granddaughter, opened the boxes, and let the concierge see everything. From that day on, though she continued to complain of her health and to recite her family's woes coupled with the troubles of the world, most of Madame D.'s questions were about Melrose. She too had a granddaughter, one nearly the same age.

Rose sighed. Dust motes fell in a slanted shaft of light across the room. She had not allowed herself to think much about those early years since she'd returned; she had been determined not to let herself be possessed by nostalgia. It was there waiting for her though, a clearly defined time falling across her life as the sun fell into the room, and no matter what she did, where she went, who she saw, her thoughts ran back to those first two years, to the Rue de l'Abbeye, the Rue de Seine, to Thomas.

She would walk every day by the Place Furstenberg admiring its wrought iron lamp, five outstretched branches holding round white globes, theatrical, absurd, and exactly right for the tiny square. Crossing the Rue de l'Echaude she could continue on two blocks to the Rue de Seine where Thomas's shop was located. He collected prints, engravings, lithographs, old ones only because, he said, one had to stop somewhere. Thomas's collection stopped at World War I. He owned nothing dated past 1918. One of her favorite posters was a piece of rationing propaganda from that period, a picture of three small children, painted in awkward stances in primary colors as if another willful child had been at work. The children faced an oval candy shop window where tiers of colored bon-bons had been piled high to catch the light in the usual French style. Above their heads ran primitively shaped letters saying, *NOUS SAURONS, NOUS ENPRIVEE.* Thomas translated for her, *We will know how to do without.* Remembering them both standing before the poster, his hand on her shoulder while he spoke, the sound of his voice, the warmth of his touch, she could only protest silently. Oh, but we don't know really! There's no way to prepare for doing without the sweets of life. It's something we learn only when we have to.

He'd inherited the business from an uncle killed in the street fighting during the liberation. Thomas, who had escaped to England with his wife and child, returned to Paris as a member of DeGaulle's army, but his wife took their daughter and went back to Grenoble. The shop had been in the family for many years. His wife refused to stay there with him. "She loves her own place, the mountains. She was born there."

Rose, waiting for him to close the shop that day, thought, I loved my place too, but I love this one more, and now I am with Thomas whose wife refused to follow him. Their separation was amiable. Thomas continued to return to Grenoble for holidays and for the long summer vacation. Later, after he and his wife were divorced, he had continued to take his daughter skiing during the Christmas season and to the Italian lakes in August. Sometimes they stayed in St. Laurent and spent part of the time on nearby Mediterranean beaches instead of going to the lakes.

To Rose their lives had a classic simplicity. She and Edward had taken two-week vacations every year, always to a different place, and always after long debates about where they should go. Should they try an island off Maine, take Phillip to Yellowstone, or go down to Mexico City? Everything was so far away from Texas. They drove around their continent taking great swathes of it in as if they had to try to see it all. Thomas and his wife had Europe for a playground, and it was compact, neatly arranged.

"Yes," he agreed, "but we French seldom use it all. I have never been to Spain."

"Well, neither have I."

"We will go. We must marry first."

"I'm not divorced yet." She was waiting then for Edward to give up. How many letters she had written, how few she'd received from him. He could write an excellent report, but his letters were dry, matter-of-fact, as if his years as a stockbroker dealing with other people's money, objectively manipulating pieces of paper, had drained away all passion. He did not plead. He said only, "Stay as long as you wish. Come home when you are ready." Fair, yes, he was quite fair, too fair.

"I am not coming back," she wrote him in her first letter. "I have been unfaithful." She committed herself on paper, wrote it, hesitating at first because those words would be so painful, and she felt she was being cowardly to write them. She should have had the courage to confront him, to say, I have been unfaithful to his face. What good would that have done? It was only the most obvious reason for her refusal to return.

He replied in an understanding tone. "Women who travel alone are sometimes tempted. One indiscretion does not necessarily lead to divorce. We have lived for twenty-five years together. I am your husband." He gave her time.

Two months later she wrote to a young lawyer, a friend of hers and Edward's, "Please persuade him to divorce me. I will not contest. I cannot return."

If he had come after her, would she have gone back to Texas with him? The gesture itself, Edward leaving everything and flying to Paris, would have appealed to her in one way, would have made her more stubborn in another. The idea of sleeping with him, as he might demand, was unbearable. Actually she couldn't imagine him there. Except for English speaking places, he hated foreign countries. Going to Mexico was always her idea. He did not like strangeness; novelty bored him. Wherever they went together he looked for something familiar, compared Mexican beef to Texas's and found it stringy, the government tyrannical, the currency inflated. He would accompany her to museums, and she'd find him an hour later waiting for her on the steps. He didn't come to France. The divorce papers were mailed to her.

She and Thomas planned to go to Italy in December. "I'm not ready," she said when he pressed her to marry him first.

"When will you be ready?"

"I don't know. You've been divorced for a while. My divorce is just now final. It's different for you."

He had come to her apartment for lunch as he did every day. After lunch they would often make love in her bedroom.

"Is that what Americans call it . . . to make love? How strange. We do not make it. It happens."

Rose laughed. "I hope so."

"You are afraid it will leave us?"

"Perhaps. I don't know."

"We are not young. We are not infatuated with the idea of love."

"I know, but—"

"If nothing else it is inconvenient not to get married. You will have to show your passport in foreign hotels and your carte d'identite."

"I didn't think you'd mind. I didn't think you'd be so—"

"Bourgeois?" Thomas laughed. "I am failing, I see, to fit your conception of a Frenchman! You forget the other side of the image. Turn around the romantic and you will discover my dark practical heart. I fear you will one day become homesick for your son, your granddaughter, your own country, and you will return to Texas. If we are not married I cannot go with you. In France we wink at liaisons, but in America, I am told, the Puritans make life difficult."

Rose adjusted the flowers in a bowl on the table. When he mentioned Puritans she'd had a flickering vision of a crowd of people dressed in stark black and white. The men wore tall hats and stared over muskets cradled in their arms. Wives in long skirts and high-necked blouses cast vindictive glances and whispered together. Not a one winked. Was that Thomas's French version of American morality? She didn't ask him.

Nor did she tell him of her own fear that she'd simply discovered him by chance and continued to cling to him because she was terrified of complete freedom. How could she ever get him to understand she had to be someone by herself with her own feelings about morality? Confused by his insistence, she wondered how much she loved him because love was something that happened, or how much was created by the necessity to love someone. She didn't know.

She refused to marry Thomas. "I was a fool!" she said out loud watching the sunlight on the black top of the piano. She had been right to wait out her uncertainty that first year. When June came around again she'd almost decided she would marry. Before she told him, however, she met Julian Roche, an old friend of Thomas's who'd known him since they were students together. They were having an aperitif one afternoon while waiting for Thomas to join them after closing hours. As usual the sidewalk was filled with a surging crowd flowing back and forth, meeting, parting, intent on some destination or merely strolling, window-shopping as they went. Rose tried to pick out the American tourists, but it seemed harder that year. They blended better.

"They've all left their cameras at home and are hiding their *Michelins*. It's easier to spot the Germans now."

"I do not want to see the Germans." Julian was brooding over his vermouth-cassis, his nose almost touching the rim of the glass. "I have seen enough of them to last forever." He was a small man, shorter than Rose. She felt he was comfortable with her only if they were seated.

"I am ridiculous. It is an old bitterness. I cannot change. I spent most of the war in a German labor camp. We will talk of something happier. You are good for Thomas. You will marry him, I hope. His wife married her lover." He paused and looked at her closely. "I give too much advice. Why? Because I never marry."

"If I do decide to marry Thomas it won't be to equal a score." She had known of Genevieve de Buvre's second marriage. Paris was a difficult place to live right after the war. The black market fed only those who could afford it, and the fuel supply was so low Thomas had burned his oil stove just in the early morning hours of the coldest days. His wife and child were more comfortable at her family's home in Grenoble. He expected them to return later. Genevieve refused to leave her home; she took a lover. She wanted the child, Therese, to herself. Thomas, refusing to make his daughter choose between them, saw Therese only during summer vacations. Gradually she slipped away from him. He blamed himself. Genevieve married her lover, stayed in Grenoble, kept her daughter there also. All this Julian told Rose; most of it she already knew. The one fact she hadn't known was that Thomas's wife married her lover. Nothing extraordinary in that. She was about to do the same thing. How much did she and Genevieve have in common? They had Thomas—one man shared by two women, his wife who turned from him to marry another while she turned from Edward to marry Thomas. The irony, the neatness of the full circle, was unbearable. It was as if her life was controlled by a malicious force which was pleased with symmetrical arrangements. Rose balked. In spite of Julian's pleadings, in spite of knowing she was choosing the more painful of two courses, she refused to marry Thomas.

When she tried to explain he laughed and told her she had a quixotic belief in free will. "All actions have been taken before, even the one you propose to take."

"Yes, I'm ridiculous," she acknowledged and heard Julian's despair echoing in her own voice.

"There must be some other reason!" Thomas went to the window and shoved the curtains to one side. He looked out at the walled garden, his back to her.

"Perhaps there is. I don't know." How could she admit to him she must have been ready for another man just as he came along? She might have told him she was beginning to be physically repelled by Edward, but that admission would have only appealed to Thomas who was already certain her desire matched his. Someone else, some other man, might have done as well. She didn't want to believe that, but it was true. And did love bind them or was it her fear of loneliness? Thomas had been lonely himself. Most of his family was gone except for a few old aunts. At least he had something he liked doing, and he was a respected art dealer. He had the shop; he had old friends. She had no ties in France. Though she spoke French, she still thought in English.

"You do not trust me." He faced her, tall for a Frenchman, dark-headed, beginning to be gray, correctly dressed in a well-tailored suit, correctly angry at her willfulness.

"I have trusted you more than I have ever trusted any man."

"Not enough to marry me, however."

He accused her of contradicting herself, of playing a role—the modern woman insisting on male freedom—of wanting to leave him, of perversity. Women were supposed to want to marry. She was not being reasonable.

Rose sat in her chair, listened, but refused to defend herself further. She hoped his anger would burn out; she waited to soothe his pride.

Then he left. The door creaked on its hinges, swung open, and he was gone. For a week she waited, without feeling much, frozen in stubbornness at first. Early every morning she walked through the Luxembourg gardens past the Medici fountain. Empty of children's boats, the usual plume of water spraying at the usual height, it too seemed frozen, a vast round mirror. Later each morning she bought the Paris edition of the *Herald* from the same kiosk, drank coffee at the same cafe, and visited a second hand bookstore where she bought copies of slightly worn English classics. Every afternoon she went to a different restaurant for lunch. At night she read Jane Austen, Dickens, or Thackeray before going to sleep. Their witty, sensible English voices both sustained and calmed her. She hadn't realized how much she missed the rhythms of the written language. The second week she began conscientiously exploring the city, riding buses or the metro to the outer limits. Then she started taking trains away to Versailles, to Malmaison, to Chartres.

She stayed in Chartres all day luxuriating in the peace, climbing to the roof for a view, sitting in a pew inside, her own discordant thoughts half-drowned in the cobalt blues of the windows, then finally forgotten while listening to a lecture on the altar screen. Undisturbed by other tourists coming and going, she sat on a wooden bench thoughtfully provided by a shop owner across the street from the facade. A small glider silently swooped down and up once more as it crossed the bit of sky framed between the two famous unmatched towers. Watching it she recognized once more the miracle of the cathedral's survival. In that moment, and every time she thought of it later, she was immensely happy.

When the train had taken her back to Paris, she began the long subway trip to the apartment. Crossing to the metro station, a ragged old man spat at her and began raving about filthy Americans who should stay at home. All this time she'd avoided self-pity; now the corrosion of despair surfaced. Loneliness oppressed and confused her.

Fleeing from the old man, she entered the wrong door to the metro during the late afternoon rush hour. Instead of going forward to St. Germain, she was being carried back to the train station. Pressed into the crowded metro, all the stations going by on the wrong side, she could think of only one thing, something her mother's cook used to say to her when she was a child. "Contrary . . . contrary . . . contrary. You don't want nobody telling you what to do. You go out and get in your own kind of trouble." Whatever the transgression—once she cut all the sashes off her dresses because she hated the knots hitting her back and more than once she skipped Latin class to go swimming in the river—Mattie's condemnation remained the same. Pushed against all the harried French people deep underground in Paris, she could still hear her disapproving voice. Rose's answer was also the same, "Better my own kind of trouble than anyone else's."

She laughed at her own trouble and at the French peering at her. When she got to the train station again she took a cab home, but was it home? She didn't hear Madame Duchard call after her when she went in, nor did she see the envelope slipped under her door. In the bedroom she kicked off her shoes and threw herself down on somebody else's bed, not even her own bedspread, in somebody else's apartment. Always she'd taken the calculated risk, looking ahead to what could possibly happen. In marrying Edward she'd known she might be making the wrong choice. He was twelve years older and far more sedate than she, yet she was adaptable. For twenty-five years she made the best of it. She left him in search of freedom only to become emotionally bound by another man, but she had to stop there. How did one get off the merry-go-round? By refusing to marry. She had not thought Thomas would leave her, had not calculated that. I'm not the first woman who's been left by a man! He is not responsible for my happiness. I am. Tomorrow I will go the American Express office and make arrangements to fly to London. How wonderful it will be to hear English spoken again by everybody, every single person on the streets, but what difference will it make if I'm thinking of Thomas. What difference language, or place, or time? I might as well be married to him. He doesn't want to even a score. I'm the one who thought of that. I can't. If he came now and asked again I couldn't. There's no necessity for it, no real one, no children. I have had one bad marriage.

"Rose, are you there?" It was Thomas outside her door.

She would have gone to London, then probably to New York, and eventually back to Texas if Thomas had not come that night.

"Every day I called, but you were not here. I wrote, but I could not wait for an answer."

"I didn't get your letter."

"Here it is. Your concierge put it under the door."

Rose held out her hand. Instead of giving her the letter, he tore it up.

"All it says is that I am coming. Where have you been?"

"Oh, everywhere, all over Paris. Today I went to Chartres."

"You have been running away, no?"

"No! Yes! I don't know."

He took both of her hands in his. "You have not changed your mind?"

"No. I can't marry again. I know it seems absurd."

"Come and live with me then. We will be absurd together."

They compromised. She lived another year at the apartment on the Rue de l'Abbeye, and when her lease expired she moved to Thomas's. Now she was back in her own house, and Theo had come to live with her. His decision to move in had been startling since she'd given the invitation abruptly in a moment of sympathy. Rose smiled to herself. The invitation hadn't included sharing her bed. After living with him a week, though, she saw they would never be at ease unless they slept together. Despite all his concern for propriety, Theo needed a woman, and he'd thought his need was indecent or, at least, immoral. She'd consoled him with tales of Victor Hugo at eighty or more still pursuing or being pursued by women. He was immensely grateful. She was strangely comforted by his lovemaking. By refusing to marry Thomas she'd evaded one circle, stepped over it, and gone on whirling in a widening spiral. What a fool she'd been to believe she could break the pattern. It was stamped on her, embossed like a monogram on layers of paper. She was to go from one man to another. It was useless to try to weigh love against necessity. For her they were equal.

Rose was talking on the phone in the kitchen when Theo got home. He tried not to listen but heard her anyway. She waved to him and said, "It's Phillip," then went on talking. They were discussing Melrose and George.

He sat down and looked about the room. Somehow today it was all so unfamiliar looking. Everything had taken on other proportions; the piano was larger, the lamps smaller, dimmer. He rested his hands on his knees. How to go about it? He couldn't simply blurt out, "Will you marry me?" What had he to offer other than respectability? When would she finish her conversation? He could hear her saying, "No need to speculate now. George is still in California. He's supposed to move into my apartment, the one over the garage, as soon as he returns."

Theo fidgeted with the crease in his trousers running his fingers down one leg until Rose came in.

"Do you think George and Melrose will get married?" he asked.

"I hope not. I like George immensely, but Melrose is too young . . . too uncertain of herself yet. She needs a few years on her own. It's lucky she found a job out there."

And we're too old. That's what she'll say. We're too old to be thinking of marriage. "Are we too old to get married?"

"Theo, are you proposing?" She looked amused.

"Yes, in my clumsy way, I am. We've already proven we can live together happily."

"I can't," she said automatically. "I can't. You are a dear, but I can't do it. I should have married Thomas and I wouldn't. I can't turn around and— Oh, you don't understand. You couldn't. The man I told you I lived with in France— We were lovers, but I refused to marry him. I should have but I wouldn't."

"Rose, it's so inconvenient—"

"Do you think we should marry for the sake of convenience?"

"At our age it's a good enough reason. That's not my only one. I love you, and it's difficult living like this."

"What did happen at the university? Did you see Gerald?"

"Yes. He invited us to dinner on Saturday, and he wants me to come back and teach again.

"How wonderful for you. Will you do it?"

"No. I haven't told him yet, but it's time for younger men to take over. Gerald says the department needs me. They probably do. If I refuse to teach, they'll find someone else who can do it just as well. I can visit anytime. Going over today I realized I could use the library when I want, go with you to listen to music, see an art show. I won't walk into classrooms to face another generation though."

"You're sure?"

"Yes." He continued as if it were the only question he really wanted to ask, "Rose, think about it . . . about marrying. You don't have to decide now. We'll talk about it later."

"All right. Still I don't think it's possible for me. I'm sixty-three and—"

He moved his hand toward her, his palm outstretched, in a gesture of negation. "Don't say it. We both know our ages." He got up. "It's a long walk back. I'd forgotten how long. I believe I'll go upstairs and rest awhile."

"Are you all right?"

"I will be." He started upstairs holding onto the banister tightly, questioning his willingness to make himself unhappy. I have everything and I still want more. I want Rose to love me instead of her memory of Thomas. If I lived to be a hundred, kept my mind, stayed in the best of health, made love every day would I still be dissatisfied? Oh yes, always some itch needing to be scratched, some new hunger. Yes. He discarded his coat and tie, unbuttoned his shirt and threw it over the foot of the bed. In front of the short mirror above his washstand he sardonically regarded his undershirt clinging to his skinny torso, his white hair, his light blue eyes. Idiot! Egotist! Self-pitying old dolt! Haven't you learned anything in seventy years on this earth? You never get exactly what you want; and if you did, you probably wouldn't like it. Well, what good does knowing it do me? He turned his back on the image in the mirror. The great difference between what his head and his heart knew was all too evident. Stretching out on the bed, he let go a muted cry like that of his old dog dreaming of the moon.

CHAPTER SEVEN

Because she'd learned late the evening before, she wouldn't phone Melrose until the next morning. Rose was up by seven wishing she could have slept later. It was five on the coast, still too early to call. She made coffee and went out to the front yard. Too early for the newspaper. Holding both hands around a coffee cup, she wandered to the side porch to sit on the glider. If she stayed near a clock, the time would never pass. Theo saw her from his window and waved. He hadn't slept well either, he said when he came down. He would fix breakfast for them both.

"I'll come inside, but I don't think I want anything," she said.

"Better to eat something. You might get weak later. Remember what going without a meal does to you."

"Oh, all right. But just toast."

They ate, both of them sitting at the kitchen table, saying little, staring at the walls opposite as if they had nothing to say. Some time before they made a rule for themselves: they would never discuss anything in the least upsetting before breakfast as they both had the same tendency to be bad tempered then, a flaw Rose readily acknowledged and Theo, when she pointed it out, recognized in himself. Before breakfast he was decidedly testy and he never meant to be. It was one of the difficulties of living with another person, the care one had to take, the time required to grow used to someone else's habits and preferences. He was a morning newspaper reader, and he wanted to read it in silence. Rose, when she read the paper, wanted to remark on stories, ask questions about people's obituaries, and complain about the lack of news from the continent. The Sunday edition of the *Times* took care of that need, and she had begun to keep some of her observations till later in the day. There was a great deal she'd missed during her years in France. He tried to fill in gaps for her until she said, “All right, Theo. Really it’s all right. I don’t have to know the whole history of the city and its population.” Her voice was so filled with laughter he didn’t feel rebuked.

Rose, watching the sun’s shadow lengthen on the wall, felt she had the hardest thing, the worst thing she’d had to do since Thomas died, and she must, absolutely must— Last night George Conway’s mother, Cynthia, phoned from Kerrville and asked her to call. Poor woman. She could hardly talk. Kevin Conway had to abruptly introduce himself when he took over the phone.

The front gate whined. Theo left the table to pick up the newspaper.

Time seemed to drag its feet when she most wanted it to run. Through the window above the kitchen sink early morning sun lit the yellow chinaberry leaves just outside the kitchen door. She’d thought she’d take that tree down and hadn’t because Melrose loved its brightness, and George remarked on its grace, particularly when all the leaves were gone and berries dangled from its dark naked branches. She’d never thought of a chinaberry tree as particularly handsome. Until Melrose and George praised it, she scorned all chinaberries as trash trees. Now hers had become a necessary splash of color and would later, sometime in November or December, become a sculpture. Now she would never replace it.

Rose walked to the door of the dining room and lifted the wall phone’s receiver. Tears made the numbers swim as she dialed. She could hear the phone ringing tiresomely over and over.

“Melrose?”

“Rosie! I would have answered sooner, but I was working. I got up real early this morning and have been in the studio ever since.”

“Is anyone with you?”

“No. George went back yesterday. Rosie, what is it?”

"I wish you weren't there alone. My dear, I've something terrible to tell you. George— George was killed His plane back to Texas crashed." The words rushed out.

Melrose kept repeating, "What?"

"The plane," Rose said again, "there was an accident, some kind of mechanical failure. It crashed in the Arizona desert somewhere near Phoenix. Everyone was killed. George's parents called and asked me to call you. Oh, Melrose, I'm so sorry."

As silently as possible, while the tears ran down her cheeks, she tried to listen while wiping her face with one hand. In the long pause, all she could hear was the sound of breathing. Rose waited. Had Melrose been standing with her back to the wall? Could she have crumpled? She wasn't given to fainting. Was she sitting on the floor staring at it. When she couldn't wait any longer, and after promising herself she wouldn't scream, that she would be calm although it was a fake calm, Rose repeated her granddaughter's name.

Melrose, her voice breaking, answered slowly, "I let him go alone, let him fly back. He was out here and I wouldn't go home with him. I didn't want to leave my job. I didn't want to leave the damn canvas I was working on."

"Oh, no! It wasn't your fault. You mustn't feel—"

"But I do. I do."

"It was an accident, Melrose. Would you like for me to come out there?"

"Rosie, what can I—? I have to— George was here for two weeks. We had a fight. It was awful. I wouldn't go back to Austin with him."

"I'll fly out there and come back with you. The Conways want to hold a memorial service for George."

"Would you? No. No, Rosie. Call here later. I can't talk any more right now."

"All right. I'll ring you again in half an hour. But remember, you must not blame yourself."

"If I'd gone with him we would have taken another plane, a later one."

"Stop it, Melrose. You cannot go on thinking like that." Rose could hear the tears beginning. "I'll call you again in a little while." She turned away from the phone and walked through the kitchen, the dining and living rooms to the side porch as if to ask the whole exterior world why.

Theo and Rose faced each other in the upstairs hall arguing. She had just talked to Marilyn who called to warn her that she and Phillip were coming a day earlier than they had originally planned. They wanted to spend more time with Melrose. The dog, too feeble now to climb the steps, sat at the bottom whining. Theo wanted to go down and comfort him, but he couldn't argue with Rose from the bottom of the steps. To go down there and look up was to declare himself defeated.

"Let Melrose have her own room," he said. "I'll go stay in a hotel, or I could even stay with the Dunhams. I'm sure they will have me."

"Theo, I've told you there's no need for that."

Rose looked exhausted. She'd been talking to Melrose, to Phillip, the Conways, Anne Tomlin, the florist, the secretary of the Episcopal church where George's memorial service would be held. Cynthia Conway had decided since most of George's friends were in Austin, the service should take place there. She would talk to the minister after Rose's conversation with the church's secretary. Cynthia knew the minister, but neither she nor Kevin could call and announce George's death all over again. Theo disliked making Rose talk to him now, but decisions remained to be made.

Homer, who always seemed to sense when something was terribly wrong, moaned pitiably.

"Hush, Homer!" Theo called to him. He didn't want to shout, but he had to make him hear, "Hush now!"

The dog, still looking up the stairs at him as if he wanted to howl, sank down on the rug.

He turned back to Rose.

"She'll feel better in a familiar place. Marilyn and Phillip will be more relaxed without me around."

"Nonsense! You won't make them nervous. Why not use the garage apartment? You knew George as well as Phillip and Marilyn, better in fact. Melrose will want to see you, and I— I need you."

She did, in an unfamiliar way, he realized. They had both watched Melrose and George and had refused to see any real danger threatening the two young people. Both of them were mistaken; in this error they had a common guilt. They had insisted on being as blind as everyone else.

"All right," he conceded, "I'll stay in the apartment. Just let me get a few of my things." He turned to go back into his room. "I don't know if I'll be of any use to you. I don't know—" He lifted some hangers of clothes out of the closet and laid them over the foot of the bed then faced her. "When we are old we die, but when the young die it seems—" He shook his head.

Rose sat down on the bed. "I know . . . more unnatural. Oh, Theo, we must help her." Tears crept silently down her cheeks.

Theo sat beside her and took her hand. "He was a fine boy. I liked him."

They sat there together for a moment then he got up, opened a bureau drawer, pickup up a clean handkerchief, and gave it to her. He got one for himself also thinking here I am, seventy years old and I don't know any new ways to comfort anybody. I'll have to depend on the old ones, on being here, on listening.

Late that night after everyone had arrived and had gone to bed, Rose moved slowly through the house locking all the doors. She never used to lock up at night when she and Edward lived together in Austin, but after years spent at Thomas's house in Paris she'd developed what Thomas called "a Mediterranean reflex." Now she locked everything, tried the handles after locking, and carried the keys latched to her belt by a ring for her tour every night. She put them down on the table beside her bed upstairs. There were only four, one for the back door, one for the front door, one to the French doors opening onto the porch, and one to her bedroom. She never used the last one. They were old brass keys bright with use. When she laid them on the table they splayed out, each one distinct in shape, shining boldly under the lamp. She had thought of herself as a chatelaine carrying the keys to her castle, a private holding, a place for herself. One could be generous yet still retreat. She had stepped outside boundaries, left the country, lived with and loved Thomas while refusing to marry him, for in the end, there was always a retreat to the hidden inner self, the self that said no, I will not be responsible for the flaws in the life of another. I cannot be held accountable for any but my own.

She sat down on the bed and looked at the keys again. With the same hand she'd locked herself away and given herself away. She had been a poor example for her granddaughter. By refraining from telling her anything or giving directions, she had failed the child. Phillip would think so. He had the same faults, the same temperament. She had told him not to play the heavy father because she recognized he was, by nature, incapable of playing such a role. And she had told herself not to interfere with Melrose and George because she couldn't be responsible, didn't want to be responsible for the morality of another generation. "But I am," she muttered harshly. I stood before her, asked her to come to see Thomas and me, paid her fares to Paris, wanted her to live with me here. Oh, why must our children and our grandchildren use us as models? Did Melrose say to herself, I will be as independent as my grandmother? Poor girl, if only she realized how dependent her grandmother was. I could have told her she was choosing the hardest way. One's own way is always the hardest. Pain doesn't show. I have a placid face. Would it have made any difference if I'd told her, if I'd chanted proverbs? You've made your bed, now lie in it. How cruel, how terribly cruel. Yet proverbs are only mean summations of experience after the fact. No one ever takes those dreary prophecies to heart while they are fulfilling them. I should have told her; My life with your grandfather was not miserable, nor did I stay with him for twenty-five years only for Phillip's sake. I was comfortable, used to being Mrs. Edward Davis. If he'd gone with me on that trip to Europe I would have probably continued to live with him. Both of my parents had died. I'd had an income of my own for sometime. Was it the freedom having the money gave me or was it restlessness? In time I would have gotten over that, but I didn't give myself time, or it wasn't given to me.

I ran toward another man, another way of life. I chose not to marry Thomas, I refused to bow a second time to convention, yet even in France where men keep mistresses I struggled against Thomas's desire for respectability. I still used Edward's name, but Thomas introduced me always as Madame de Buvre. We fought for months over that. When his daughter married, he went alone to the ceremony in Grenoble. I never met her, nor did I meet any of his family. Except for you, he never met any of mine. We had elaborate rules. I would not go back to America if he wouldn't come with me, and he wouldn't. Neither one of us ever left the house without saying exactly where we were going. Every weekday morning he left for the shop knowing my schedule for the day. When I took short trips by myself, the telephone bill was enormous because I called Thomas every night. Yes, we were happy. We had to work so hard to be, we might as well have been married.

Would it have made any difference if I'd told Melrose? Did she consciously choose to experiment or was it simple inclination? What difference does it make? By choice or accident we've come to the same grief.

On her way back from San Francisco, Melrose stopped in Phoenix. There was nothing to see at the crash site, she told her grandmother, nothing except burned ground; a big char, black and brown, marked the earth. Desolation. Cacti and desert sand would drift over it again soon. Investigators were keeping the pieces of the plane, and bits of strewn baggage until they were sure of the cause of the accident though what difference that would make, she didn't understand. The cabby who'd driven her out from the airport said investigators always kept the pieces.

The Conways would go to Phoenix a week or two later. George's mother had said they planned to erect a tombstone for him at their plot in Kerrville's cemetery.

"Isn't that strange," Melrose demanded, "when there's nothing to bury!"

Rose tried to answer her. "I've seen it happen before. Perhaps his parents want to commemorate him this way, or they're doing it as a record for future generations."

"Oh, Rosie! George has no future! What good will it do to have his name written in stone?"

"It must comfort his parents somehow, just to say he was here." Rose blinked back tears and opened both her arms.

Her granddaughter turned away and ran upstairs.

She had been acting the same ever since George's memorial service at the small Episcopal church near the university. Mrs. Conway, thinking it might please Melrose, had said he'd gone to nursery school there. Hearing this and other simple memories his mother had, the details she'd never known—the way he'd mispronounced strawberries as "strawbellies," how long he wore braces, the cardboard fort he'd built when he was nine—served only to intensify Melrose's sorrow.

Her reaction puzzled Rose at first then she saw Melrose was going to continue to refuse comfort from anyone. The guilt could not be shared, nor could the loss be measured by anyone except herself. Determined on her independence, she would slowly, perhaps, recognize the selfishness of grief.

Theo looked over the agent's shoulder to the travel poster on the wall. It was the familiar picture of Neuschwanstein, Ludwig II's fairy-tale castle which he insisted on bringing to life in the 19th century long after the age of castle building was finished. Tall, white, round-towered, a place where Cinderella could have danced, a backdrop for a Wagnerian opera, fake yet terribly satisfying to Ludwig, the overwrought romantic. Theo had no desire to see anything more of Neuschwanstein than the poster. He was happy it existed; he found it comforting that Teutonic madness could develop into an obsession for castles and costumes rather than conquests and brown shirts. To think on Ludwig often led him to visions of the Second World War, to the other madman and concentration camps. No, he preferred Germany as Miss Ney had left it. He would not go there at all. A leisurely trip beginning in France was his preference and Rose's. He waited for the agent to confirm their bookings on the ship.

"One stateroom, October 16?" The man's voice was as well-modulated as a radio announcer's. He must have been trained to soothe demanding people.

"Yes, that's correct."

They would travel together though she would not marry him. He'd really thought perhaps she would. He had hoped, asked. Hadn't he known in some part of his mind, that Rose would never marry again? It was simpler for her not to. For him it wasn't. Either way his children would consider him hopelessly lost in his dotage. He'd have to put up with that. The letters he'd written had not been easy. It was like confessing a crime, stating bluntly, "Rose Davis and I have decided to go to Europe." He'd thought of telling them he'd asked her to marry him and ended by saying nothing on the subject. He couldn't explain her refusal in a letter. How could they understand she wouldn't marry him because she hadn't married someone else? Actually he didn't owe them an explanation. They would have to endure his eccentricity. Perhaps they wouldn't think of his and Rose's union as anything more than that. After all they had lived in the world for a while now. Ted and Kenneth were grown men; surely they had seen all sorts of combinations. And when he thought of the variety of matches, including those of people who lived in communes, his and Rose's was almost ordinary.

"I'll pay you now." He pulled out his checkbook and wrote a check for his half. Taking Rose's signed check from his wallet, he filled in the agency's name and pushed it across the counter.

It was not easy to leave the country although the decision was made. Rose decided to go without apparent effort. All she had to do was to change her mind, to declare she was not prepared to come home and stay after all. For him it was harder to overlook the obvious reasons for staying at home. Getting a new passport was a nuisance as his birth certificate had long ago vanished. Making trips to city offices, standing in lines, explaining himself . . . all of the arrangements were tiring. Gradually he saw he was loosening himself from his known place, preparing to go into the unknown. He would be needlessly uncomfortable in strange cities; he valued his own bed, and he did not look forward to fatigue caused by overexcitement. Gerald said he wanted old stones, but Theo felt that the accretion of years in European cities might overstimulate him. He would never be alone. There wasn't a park bench in Paris he wouldn't share with LaFayette or Ben Franklin, and they would be crowded off by others; Voltaire, Robespierre, Napoleon, Louis XIV, St. Joan, Charlemagne, all of them shouting, "Listen to me! Listen to me." And if he wasn't listening to one of the grander ones he would be hearing the whispers of unknown peasants, street-fighters, dreamers saying, "It was like this. . . ." He would have to give up his old ghosts at the Ney museum for older ones. Never mind, he counseled himself, just beyond chosen solitude lies a vast stretch of desert loneliness, and by going with Rose I escape that. If this is escapism, better to escape. Only slightly guilty over the pleasure he'd claimed for himself, Theo pocketed their tickets.

An immense feeling of freedom swept over him; without thinking he traced the pattern of a miniature waltz step on the floor. He would go now to the men's store and buy winter clothes to take with him. His news would make Gordon Tanner happy. Gerald already knew they were going. He hadn't told Tim yet, nor Ricardo. He dreaded telling him. No use promising he'd be back. Ricardo wouldn't believe him anyway, and he couldn't promise. He planned, yes, Rose and he planned to return. Still there was no way of knowing. Death was a certainty he faced, but he no longer sat waiting for it. On the other hand, small uncertainties about travel schedules were pleasantly novel.

He and Rose would go to Paris for a while, then to Italy when it got colder. On the way to Venice they would stop by Grenoble. She wanted to see Thomas de Buvre's grave, a desire he understood though he thought he would wait for her at the hotel. He had visited Kate's grave the day after George's memorial service and tried to think what she would have said about the life he was leading. He thought, in the long run, she wouldn't condemn him. He'd attempted to explain to Melrose that the dead do not reproach the living. It was too soon for her to find any comfort in that idea. Without returning to San Francisco, she gave up her apartment and sold her car. Friends there were keeping her pictures until she could bear to look at that group of pictures again. Her grief touched them all. She was staying at home with Rose now, another reason they were leaving.

Last night Rose said she'd reached a decision. " Melrose has had only a little while now. Unless we go away I'm afraid she'll stay, and it isn't good for her. I would ask her to go with us. That wouldn't help her either."

"Perhaps she only needs more time," he said.

"Yes, time to herself, time to get out and be with other young people. At least I can leave her my car. She must do something for herself now."

"She's afraid."

"I know," Rose said.

Melrose spent most of the day outside in the garden or walking in the neighborhood. Rose's house was practically her private island. Sometimes she read; sometimes she wrote a few letters. She spoke to her friends when they called however she seldom called anyone. A week was all she would spend with her parents in Dallas. She wouldn't even let Rose ask someone to come keep her company, nor would she paint, and she'd quit her job at the advertising agency in San Francisco after her leave of absence ran out.

Theo didn't know what to advise. Whenever he tried to talk to her she'd say, "I shouldn't have insisted on going to California. If I hadn't— I thought I had to get away." The slightest memory of any of the circumstances of George' s death made her cry. He'd put his arm around her shoulders and wait for her to stop. Her thoughts remained the same; she continued to judge herself guilty.

Finally he knew he must try to stop her and raised his voice above hers. "If you hadn't! If you hadn't been born! If George hadn't got on that plane! Life's an accident!"

"Not anymore," she said in a wry voice.

"Well, nobody knows who they'll be born to. We don't pick our parents, and we don't know when we'll die." I live, he thought, on the edge of life, the far edge now. For seventy years I've taken the same risks as everyone else does, and I've not been struck by lightning, cars, or falling limbs. I have not lost my sanity, and my health, except for my back and a touch of arthritis, is remarkable. I've walked the edge every day. I look forward to tomorrow, all senseless to Melrose. Why should she find any relief in the fact of my survival? It is her own she seeks reason for. He walked on down the street toward the store thinking, as he often did, on the uselessness of rationality.

Gordon was delighted to see him again and to know he was going to Europe.

"Why don't you wait and buy your suits in London? My uncle knows a fine tailor there."

"I suppose I could, however I don't know when I'll get to London exactly, and when I do I don't intend to spend my time shopping. The lady I'm traveling with will probably do enough of that."

"Women," sighed Gordon immediately drawing them together into the brotherhood of bored, patient men who sat on hard chairs or escaped to browse through bookstores while their wives tried on clothes.

When he'd finished making his purchases Theo was dismayed at first at the thought of carrying them all to the house. He should have driven Rose's car. Of course he could phone her to come, or he could take a cab, but it was a cool day and he'd looked forward to walking back. The store, he was certain, was too small to offer delivery service. He wouldn't embarrass Gordon by asking for it. Well, if he couldn't carry his clothes a few blocks home he had no business hoping to carry them over half of Europe. When he left he was trying to adjust the balance of weight among two boxes and a sack. Before he'd walked three blocks he'd vowed to travel light and after six he was wondering if he might possibly kick the larger box along in front of him at least until his arms were rested, or he ran into something. When he started down a small hill he dropped the larger box on the ground and gave it a gentle shove with one foot. It slid along easily.

Rose walked out to the back garden. Melrose seemed to be watching the birds bathing in the fountain on the back wall. They were splashing about so they were flinging water out of the basin. Rose doubted her granddaughter was actually seeing much of anything. In the last few weeks it was as if her well-trained eyes no longer fastened on objects or noticed the play of light and shadow at all. Food was no distraction. Slender already, she'd grown so thin her shirt sleeves drooped from her shoulders.

"Theo called a little while ago. He was able to book passage for us."

"Where?"

"We're going first to France, Melrose. We told you the other night."

"I forgot."

Rose sat down beside her wishing she could give her some of her own energy, that it came in units like blood. Whenever she saw Melrose, she was reminded of the weariness of her own grief, the long months of tears and numbness. She looked at her granddaughter slumped in the chair; she was way too thin, too pale. "What will you do?" she asked abruptly.

"I don't know, stay here I guess. If you'll let me."

"Alone?"

"Why not?"

"You will be— It would be too lonely. You can't become a recluse."

"Why not? I wouldn't be less lonely anywhere else."

"You have a lot of living to do. You can't sit here the rest of your life."

"What do you think I should I do, Rosie?"

The question was of no real interest to her, Rose could tell. It was only something to say, something to hush her up. "I can't tell you what to do. You're the only one who's capable of deciding on that."

"I don't know if I can go back to San Francisco."

"Go somewhere else then."

"I'm not sure the place makes that much difference anymore. I don't know if I'll ever be able to paint again. It seems so useless to me now."

"Any kind of work seems futile sometimes."

"Who needs another picture?"

Rose, refusing to be drawn into a fruitless argument about the demand and supply of art, said only, "Melrose, you're a good painter." Naturally there were lots of others, but that was no reason to quit. She'd had some encouragement, won a prize, and sold two pictures in California. Apparently none of that made the slightest difference to her now.

"You don't like my pictures, do you, Rosie?"

Thankful for the animating spark of anger, Rose retorted, "What does my liking them have to do with your painting?" There was a great deal she didn't know about contemporary painting. She'd looked at lot of pictures by Braque and Picasso, had seen some by Miro in Paris. She'd even noticed de Kooning's work, but she hadn't looked at a lot of what was going on in the U.S. since she'd returned. She smiled. "Your grandmother is something of a Philistine. You know, though, Theo isn't. Ever since that show at the museum he's been curious about new painters. We've been over to the art museums at the university several times."

"Oh Rosie, I used to think you were the only older person I knew who wasn't petrified." She paused for a moment then asked, "Will you and Theo ever marry?"

"I don't think so. I'm sixty-four now. It's too late for me to change my ways."

"I'll never marry."

"Don't say that. You're only twenty-two. You've got years ahead of you."

A car stopped at the back gate, and they overheard Theo thanking someone.

A woman's voice replied. The gate was pushed open and a long box shoved through followed by Theo carrying his other purchases. He put the second box and a big sack on top of the one on the ground.

"Helen Abercrombie caught me coming home kicking my clothes downhill," he explained. "So she insisted on giving me a lift."

"Did you tell her what you were buying all those clothes for? I hope you did," Rose said.

Theo laughed. "Yes. I told her we were sailing later this month. I'd better tell May Dickens too. She'll be upset if she finds out I told someone else first. Helen said she hoped I wouldn't get seasick. She always does. And before I could mention any of our plans, she was prophesying a Third World War would break out in Europe." He turned to pick up his bundles. "I don't know what I'm laughing about. She may very well be right. She's afraid of war there and revolution here. I told her I'd been something of an expert on the American revolution, and I'd hate to miss one here."

Rose was inside giving Michael Hallaran a recorder lesson, teaching him songs from Shakespeare's plays. Megan had learned the words to one and was singing, "*When that I was a little tiny boy. With a heigh-ho, the wind and the rain*—- Go on Michael! Why'd you stop?"

"You are not a little tiny boy!"

"It's only what the song says," Rose interrupted. Michael was going through an extremely literal phase.

"Let's begin again." She hit the first note on the piano.

"I want to sing the rest of the song!" Megan's voice rose in a soprano screech.

"The next note is hard to hit, you dumb-dumb! You don't know one note from another. All you know is words and you can't even read them good!"

"I am not a dumb-dumb!" Megan screamed.

Rose began playing loud, rumbling chords on the piano. Every time they quarreled she created background music. Eventually both children got interested in the reflections of themselves in the music and stopped fighting. Theo had asked her if it wouldn't be simpler to tell them to hush or to send one of them home. She agreed it probably would be, but she enjoyed inventing the accompaniment. By now she'd worked out several variations on a dissonant theme.

Ricardo arrived just as Michael began again. With the Hallaran children there, Theo decided he'd better tell the boy he was leaving before Michael and Megan blurted it out. He hoped they hadn't heard Ricardo coming in the gate. He'd stopped in front of the lily pond as usual to watch the gold fish. They were hard to see as the leaves of the plants covered almost the whole surface, and beneath the leaves the water shone black.

"It's time to clean this out again."

He knelt by the side of the pool and tugged at the thick leaves pushing them apart. Bubbles rose to the surface.

"I wonder why they are round? Why can't bubbles be squares or triangles?"

Theo mumbled something about air pressure which he realized he didn't understand too well himself. He wasn't good at scientific explanations and Ricardo's questions frequently astounded him. The world is round, balloons are usually round, bubbles are round; but the boy's mind was not fettered by these assumptions. He suggested as he usually did that Ricardo either look it up in an encyclopedia or ask his science teacher. Staring down at him Theo realized he'd grown a lot that summer. When he stood up his head came almost to his teacher's chin. Ricardo would be nine in December. They had thought of spending Christmas in Rome.

"I must tell you something." It was a bad beginning. He'd never found any easy words for difficult situations. "Mrs. Davis and I are going on a trip. We're going to Europe in two weeks. We'll cross the Atlantic in a ship."

"When do you return?"

"We haven't set that date."

"Will you come back ever?"

"We plan to. You see, I've never been. I went to England once, but I've never been to France really, or Italy, or any of the other countries, not to mention the eastern half of the world."

"You have been to Mexico."

"Yes. That's closer though. It's on the same continent, you know. Perhaps we'll get to Spain or even Greece."

"There are a lot of countries," said Ricardo as though he was reciting a fact newly learned.

Theo jerked his head up. They had talked about the Greek heroes, the boy read him newspaper stories from all over the world. Now it sounded as if he'd never had the slightest concept of the earth as a planet divided into oceans, continents, and countries. How much do we teach when we teach, he wondered, and almost laughed aloud at himself for wondering. He'd been thinking about that ever since he began teaching, and here he was facing perhaps his last student and the same question. Ricardo could have been so intent on simply absorbing the language that he'd only learned words and a little sentence construction. Oh, surely he was beyond that! Surely some information had been transmitted! Possibly he was judging too much from the boy's tone of voice.

"Do you. . . ? Is there a globe at your school?" He remembered the ones he used to see in the school rooms of his childhood. They were usually up in front of the room, up front and to the right. The teacher would have to call the whole class to come closer to look at it. What did they use now, slides and projectors? Assigned TV programs?

" We look things up on it all the time. I found Austin."

"Tomorrow find Paris, and Athens, and Saigon, and. . . ." His mind went spinning around the globe, "Tokyo, and Melbourne, and Seattle."

"Why? I know where they are already."

"Good."

"Except for Mel—?"

"M-e-l-b-o-u-r-n-e." Theo spelled it.

"OK. I find it tomorrow."

"Well, don't wait until you're as old as I am to see some of these places."

"How much does it cost?"

"Depends on how you go. Students usually get by cheaply."

"How much?"

"I don't know exactly. One of my students lived for three months abroad on seven hundred dollars. That was years ago though. He spent a lot of time in Spain. It's cheaper there."

"We do not have seven hundred dollars."

"When you are older you can work and save it."

"If I did I would buy a motorcycle."

No! Theo wanted to shout and didn't, for what right had he to condemn the boy's desire? "Maybe," he hesitated then went on, "Your parents will think your education is more important."

"Maybe. Quien sabe?" He shrugged.

Damn the fatalism! Damn all the false gods who had nothing to offer but shiny working parts. How many generations would it take to eradicate unquestioning submission to machines? How long will it take before men can stand on their own feet without motorcycles or cars to proclaim their manhood? Go on and get your motorcycle. I'll get you to Europe someday. I'll call my lawyer, yes, and arrange to leave something in my will. Designate it for travel only. I'll have to tell the boys. They may not like it. I don't want them taking Ricardo to court after I'm gone. Best they know about it beforehand. They've never been greedy. Everything else goes to them. I'll have to go downtown to sign a codicil at the lawyer's office, and I'll need to write Ted and Kenneth. More letters to write. Bother.

He wandered over to the steps and sat down. Ricardo followed him.

"Who will look after the dog?"

"I don't know. Homer's old and nearly deaf. I've been worrying about what to do with him."

"I will look after him."

"All right. Thank you. I'll be happy for you to have him. He knows you. I was thinking I might send him to my son in California, and I was afraid he might not survive the trip."

"Where is he?"

"Asleep in the sun by the kitchen door as usual. He's not much of a dog for a boy, Ricardo. He's so old he sleeps most of the day."

"I know. My mother will like him. She hates barking dogs."

"This one is inclined to sniff and bark around a new place until he gets used to it but it doesn't take him long." Theo remembered the first nights he'd spent in Rose's house, Homer barking, Rose in her nightgown. How excited he'd been at the sight of her. He was still a man, he reassured himself, wondering at the same time if the tales of Parisian bordellos were true. And what if they were? He couldn't imagine knocking at the door of one. Oh, Lord, he prayed, let me not become a dirty old man! It's past the time for me to be having thoughts like these at all. I always believed sexual needs ebbed away as the years went by, but here I am, a young man in an old husk. If only Rose hadn't refused his offer of marriage, if they had met some other place, some other time, if— No, there was only one time they could have met and loved each other, now when they were old.

Ricardo had gone around to the back of the house looking for Homer. Theo got up to check on them. Passing by the doors leading in from the veranda, he stopped to listen to Megan and Rose singing while Michael played:

Fortune my foe, why dost thou frown on me?
And will thy favors never greater be?
Wlit thou I say, forever breed me pain?
And wilt thou ne'er restore my joys again?

Background music for the maundering thoughts of an old man. Perhaps he should take up the recorder! He was sure he could do as well as Michael. He'd missed the D sharp again.

CHAPTER EIGHT

Almost mid-October and still in the high eighties every day. Theo was certain it used to be cooler sooner when he was a boy. Maybe he wanted to think that; maybe weather memory, like so much of the rest of memory was selective. He hadn't compared notes on this with Rose. They had decided not to go around talking about how much better things used to be, but now and then he took pleasure in private reminiscence about the days of his youth. He knew he used to rake leaves in October; now everyone waited till November. Tim agreed with him. At the noon hour on his Saturday at the museum, he'd gone out to the big live oak tree behind the museum to sit down on the grass beside him. If Tim was surprised to see him there, he didn't show it. They both opened their lunches and ate while talking about how the smell of burning leaves, forbidden by city ordinance now, had been the signal for another season.

"I make a little pile of leaves and burn them in the back yard just to smell them," Tim confessed. "So far nobody's minded. Do you think they'd make you do time over leaf burning?"

"I might try that some day," said Theo as he leaned back against the tree trunk. "Probably they just fine people."

"That's what I'm talking about," Tim said. "Doing the time, not the fine."

Theo smiled. Then, because he hadn't been able to think of any other way to bring up the subject, told him abruptly, " I'm leaving this job."

"You quitting?"

"Yes. I'm going to Europe for a while with Mrs. Davis, the lady I share the house with."

"Hmn." Laughter sparkled in Tim's eyes. When Theo moved in with Rose, one of Tim's nephews who had a pickup truck helped him box books, and with another young man, carried the few pieces of furniture he'd kept to its new location.

"She . . . ah, she refuses to marry me."

"That's too bad."

"Yes. Well she's not," he paused searching for words. "She's not a conventional sort of woman. She's been married before, but she won't marry again."

"Well some is the regular sort, and some is not. Take the one who lived right here. She wasn't the usual sort of woman. The lady who works in the museum says Miss Ney left her husband at home and moved here to build this place. She camped out right here on the grounds, lived in a tent watching the house get built. I guess she thought she could hurry it up just by being here."

Tim pulled a huge piece of chocolate cake out of his sack.

"Look at that! Ruby made it yesterday. I bet them kids will eat it all up by the time I get in tonight. There's no such thing as a leftover in our kitchen. A ant couldn't make a living there. You want some?"

Theo nodded, and Tim handed him half of the piece of cake.

"When are youall leaving?"

" Soon. October I'm told it's a fine time to travel. I don't know exactly when we'll come back. When it gets too cold maybe. We could spend the winter in one of the warmer countries though." He ate his cake, thankful that Tim had offered it, thankful that the subject had been so skillfully changed.

"I got used to you being here."

"I got used to being here myself. I'll miss the museum, and I'll miss you."

"Probably they will hire some bossy old lady, and I will have to tip-toe around here watching my step."

"Maybe not. I wonder—" He was thinking of Melrose. Would she like to come out there on Saturday mornings? It would be something for her to do—not enough. A pleasant job for an elderly man, perhaps not for a young girl.

"You coming next Saturday?"

"No. This will be my last day."

" I don't guess it'll hurt none for you to see some of the world."

He sounded so fatherly Theo asked slyly, "You think I'm old enough then?"

"I don't know. You might wait another ten years or so." Tim laughed.

Theo laughed with him thinking, it's a shame I may never see him again. I've just begun to know him, and there's so much about his life I don't know. He's been my emissary from the other half of the city. My only real knowledge of life in East Austin has come through him.

"You write me some postcards?"

"Of course. And if we settle down for a while in any place, I'll send you my address." But it won't last. A few cards, a letter or two. Oh, the people I've lost contact with in my life! How many? I don't want to try to remember. He pushed the thought from his mind before he could begin listing names. No need to start. They had lost contact with him as well except perhaps through Christmas cards. Didn't Marshall Stevens write from Barcelona last year?

In spite of his intention, he began to remember names of people he knew who lived in Europe. He might see Marshall. They had been students together at Cornell. Both of them left Austin to go up there. What did I do with last year's cards? Threw them out when I moved in with Rose, that's what. Humph! I must have his address somewhere—that old address book of Kate's if I can find it. Why is it that I, a historian, have so little personal history? I'll leave no boxes of papers to be sifted through, no old letters, very few documents. Had to go to the public health department to get a copy of my own birth certificate for the passport. I didn't even save that box of reprints of my published articles. The collected works of Theo Isaac. Scholarly dust. Obscurity's footprints! I got tired of going through other people's papers and threw away my own. What did I keep? Pictures of the boys when they were young, of Kate when she was a bride, of my parents and hers—faded now. The family Bible. I ought to send it to Kenneth. He's the only one even vaguely interested. Thank God there's usually one child in a family who wants to know something of the past. It's a meaningless recitation of names unless one has some feeling for history. My grandsons are the physical embodiment of this country's expansion. They may know this one day, but by then will they care that their great-great-great grandfather fought and died in an unnamed skirmish in 1777, or that one of their great-grandmothers forgot where she buried her silver teapot in 1863? I suppose they won't care a great deal. Kate's things I sent to them will help them remember us at least. After a while furniture begins to stand for people; "grandfather's desk, grandmother's clock, mother's chair." Utilitarian memorials. Kate's address book could be in the box with the pictures I saved. Strange to be able to remember those scraps of paper at all when I so often forget what I did five minutes ago.

He'd left Tim and was inside the museum walking through the rooms looking at what Elisabet Ney had left, her work mainly, her house; the museum was her monument. There were a lot of little objects collected in the west room. He hadn't been in there for months. He went through the studio full of Europeans to the last tiny room; it had been her sitting room. Dark as a tomb, the walls, painted a putty color a third of the way up, changed to black with a red border at top. Had it been necessary for her to escape from gleaming day, from well lit spaces, and stark white marble to the dark? Or was she trying to bring decor from another country to Texas, something seen on her earlier trips before she left Germany when she traveled to Italy or Greece? Hanging on either side of the west door were two clumsily painted strips of canvas. On a pink background were vases twined with misshapen ivy that crawled out of them and down the length of the strips to end in masks—neither comic nor tragic. If the masks had ever stood for anything, hack work had smoothed away their significance. Now they appeared simply indifferent. How could Ney have bought those strange canvas pieces when she demanded so much of herself as an artist? Perhaps someone gave them to her, some friend who would notice if they were not hanging. Perhaps one of the caretakers had chosen to put them up later.

Next to one of the canvas strips, was a bust of Lorne, her surviving child, done when he was fifteen, a beautiful boy, whose character was evidently still forming. There was no trace of sullenness or rage, no hint of the struggle between the domineering mother and the son who naturally resisted her will. She'd portrayed him as a sensitive romantic, his head slightly bowed, when he was right in the middle of a miserable adolescence. Lorne had been made to wear dresses, kept away from other children his age, and taught at home until he was in his teens.

Theo shook his head as he thought of all the tales about Miss Ney and her sons. The most startling one—she'd cremated the body of her first child, Arthur, in the fireplace at Liendo—continued to give him goose flesh at the base of his neck even when he told himself he could not believe it. There were all kinds of reasons given for the act. Because the baby died of diphtheria, their doctor demanded it to prevent spreading disease; public cremation wasn't available; they didn't know where they would be buried, and they wanted the child buried with them. But the body of a child nearly two years old burned in the fireplace! An invention surely, a tale started by someone with a Gothic imagination. Whatever reasons they had for the cremation, tales about it could not be erased. Foreign visitors, Germans mostly as he recollected, might come just to see the studio and the casts. But sixty years after Miss Ney had died, and Edmund was laid beside her with stones erected on both their graves at Liendo, local people who came to the museum, especially the older ones, still talked about the cremation of the baby in the fireplace. They couldn't give it up; it was too memorable, too horrifying, and whether they admitted it or not, most people enjoyed a shock of horror now and then . . . as long as it wasn't their own.

Of all those affected, the one Theo pitied most was Dr. Montgomery. It was not easy to be the husband of an unconventional wife, especially one who clung to her own name and, by all reports, was too determined to raise their son her own way. There must have been times when Montgomery had to intervene, times when he knew other ways were better. What about Rose and Phillip? She might be unconventional now, but her son was twenty-five, married, and had a small child before she left Edward Davis. Phillip, the psychiatrist, was in the business of helping others adjust. Of course, Rose's transgressions were minor compared to Elizabet's deviations. Surely there was a need for rule breakers. There were too many rules. Theo stared at the face of the fifteen-year-old boy who fought for his own way and found he was caught in paradox again; a great deal of lip service was paid to individualism while the ultimate boundaries of the permissible remained the same. One should not drink away a life, let illegitimate children go unacknowledged, allow bills to remain unpaid. People did those things all the time however, and some of them like Lorne suffered personally and publicly.

He turned from the bust of Lorne to look at a glass case containing bits of memorabilia, collected no doubt by people who couldn't sort the important from the unimportant. Pitchers that Ney had used stood next to a book by Schopenhauer, the nihilist and well-known woman hater. He'd inscribed it for her lovingly, an odd contradiction, but he must have admired her—a woman, an artist, willfully determined to be a sculptor. On the top shelf there was a collection of small studies: "Study for Statue of Count Engebert von der Mark, Ancestor of the Prussian Royal Family. Statue Destroyed in the Bombing of Münster, Westphalia During WW II," Theo muttered the words typed on a card leaning against the figure. Cloaked, covered in knight's armor, holding a shield and a sword—sturdy old anachronism, destroyed in the bombing—lived by the sword, died by air attack. So did the soldier next to him. As though he'd been commanded to, Walter von Plattenburg stood "at ease" still encased in armor and clutching his sword. Theo imagined them sternly admiring the creation of their state from the facade of a government building or perhaps waiting quietly in a courtyard to be knocked off their pedestals and crumbled. The boundaries of the permissible were erased by war.

Leaving the gloomy little room, he returned to the large studio to touch the statue of Prometheus once more on his stained leg where so many others had touched him. Ney had not shown him as a suffering god; there was no intended parallel between Christ and this Prometheus. This was the last of the Titans, the Prometheus of Aeschylus, humanity opposing the brute strength of Zeus, man versus tyranny, a rebel insisting on man's right to the power of fire, that most dangerous gift. Whether she intended it or not, the idea of Prometheus as a Christ figure imposed itself. Ricardo, with his picture of the bleeding heart of Jesus, was proof of that connection.

He turned from Prometheus to the cast of Fredrich Wöhler, the chemist who, with his long thin face, looked like the noblest Roman of them all. Age and air, plus some chemical combination of elements in the plaster, had stained part of his nose green. Impervious to humiliation, Wöhler's streak was but one more patrician distinction. Theo nodded briefly toward him thinking with such a face, the scientist should have been a king. He expected to see that kind of face again engraved on old coins or portraits perhaps in Italy, and although real aristocracy was out of style, there was still a chance left for nobility of spirit. He'd never thought of himself as a man born too late. Soaked in history as he was, he was, he remained a man of his own time. He knew too much nostalgia for a better past was a fault of the old, one he must guard against.

Oh, I'm not dismissing you, he spoke to the assembled nobles silently. You are relevant. I've spent forty years in your service, making such as you and George the Third, that bad example of a king, relevant, telling students that the past and present coincide.

Sensing movement in the next room he looked through the doorway to see Melrose standing by his desk. At least she was there . . . a good sign. She hadn't been out to the museum since April, the day she came to collect her prize money. For the last few weeks she had refused to leave the house. He tried not to show surprise. After saying hello he commented, "It's too bad there's not a picture in the place right now except for these old portraits." With one hand he gestured toward them.

"I didn't come to see anything," she said. "I . . . I came to ask you something." She sat in his chair with her head in her hands. "Oh! Why do changes have to be made? Why can't I just be still? I can't bear the idea of going back to an apartment in San Francisco. I don't want to go anywhere. What I want to do is stay at Rosie's a while. Do you think she'll let me?"

"Why shouldn't she?"

"She's got an idea that I ought to leave the scene here, that I've got to get back out in the world. I need more time. I'd like to be here . . . alone. My parents are great, but they would only be dragging me out to places, introducing me to people. I need a certain kind of loneliness. Do you understand? If I could I'd stay out here, sleep in that old hammock."

"Oh, don't try that, please. It's so old, you'd only fall through."

All those plaster casts and gray white sculptures would look so ghostly in the moonlight. Theo shivered slightly. Rose's house was familiar . . . secure, and it would be empty. Melrose had known George when she lived there, had seen him often in the house, in the garden. "You want me to speak to her?"

She nodded. "I've tried, but Rosie doesn't hear what she doesn't want to hear. She won't really listen."

They started home together. Melrose said little. Her long blonde hair, hanging loose on either side, half hid her face.

"Will you be able to work at the house?" He wondered if she might not be almost too sheltered there, too protected behind the walls surrounding the place.

"I don't know. Some days I don't even feel anything. Others I feel too much. I react to everything, and I can't sort any of it out."

"That happens after weeks of grief. Gradually ordinary life takes over. Sometimes I think that's what saves us . . . ordinariness. You have to deal with it, to eat, to comb your hair, to go to the grocery." He'd never given words to this feeling before, never acknowledged the necessity of routines had helped him come back to the living world, but for him, it was true. For Melrose, he didn't know.

"I don't want it to. I don't want to feel ordinary again! If I do, it'll mean I've given up . . . I've forgotten him."

He remembered that, the clinging to grief, the fear he might lose it, and if he did, his love for his wife would also diminish. It hadn't. Nor had loving Rose altered his love for Kate. He was quite capable of loving any number of people. He almost laughed aloud at the idea of his heart's capacity to expand, but Melrose might be hurt by laughter. Instead he mentioned how the leaves were turning so slowly this year.

She didn't seem to hear.

Actually, when he reconsidered, they were hardly turning any more slowly than usual. It only seemed that way some years. Fall had seldom been a real season in Austin. Maybe that was why he and Tim needed a certain smell to signal it. Otherwise it was just a dallying drift of leaves through days so warm that fall in Austin would be summer to someone from the north. Here the lantana bloomed purple, orange, and white in everyone's beds, and the wildflowers, so many yellow ones he could never remember their names, flourished in yards and ditches.

Theo walked on silently beside Melrose. It was hard to know how to help people in mourning. He found Rose in the back yard standing quite still holding onto a rake. She was inclined to use one when she got upset, when her world needed straightening. It was as if she wanted to physically clear the space around her so there were no barriers between her interior muddles and an exterior place she might push them, like worry itself was a tangled heap of broken objects or a bundle of dirty clothes. Slowly she began raking a thin layer of elm leaves in a circle around her. When she saw him, she smiled and let the rake fall beside her.

"Melrose," he said and turned to see she'd already gone inside.

Rose waited in the circle she'd raked. "I'm glad she walked over there to see you. She's been living here like a nun, Theo. She wants to cloister herself behind the walls of this house, behind the garden walls too. I can't agree to that."

"Mourning takes different forms."

"She's too young to shut herself away." Rose gazed toward the cherubs on the fountain. She'd always thought they were comic; now they appeared merely foolish.

"I don't think it will be for long." The tentative sound of his voice echoed his doubts, so he added, "Surely she'll get tired of being here by herself."

"It's not normal."

"When did normality start making any difference to you?"

"Theo!" She sank down to the edge of the fountain, her fingers laced under her chin, elbows on knees. "It's just that I've always encouraged Melrose to do what she wanted. Now I don't think I should."

"Perhaps she somehow knows what's best for her."

"No she doesn't. She only does what she pleases. She's too much like me." She began tracing a continually disappearing pattern in the water with her fingers.

"Humph!" Theo turned his gaze toward a mass of dark pink bougainvillea, still alive, still rioting by the fountain. Tissue paper flowers, fragile as the life he and Rose had made. A quarrel could destroy it. She was being wrong-headed. Well if their arrangement couldn't withstand argument, it was altogether too weak to survive a long trip. Oh, I am so sensible, the most sensible old man I know. How I hate quarreling!

"Melrose is not like you." His voice was quiet but decisive.

"Yes she is." Rose shook her hand and dried it on the bottom of her smock. How could he made such a pronouncement? He knew too little about both of them. "For one thing, she's wary of marriage."

"After a certain age nearly everyone is." He smiled and cocked his head just a bit to one side.

"She's self-indulgent."

"So are we all. We only pretend not to be."

"I've spoiled her."

"For God's sake, Rose, you are her grandmother. That's your right."

" Oh, that's just what everyone says about grandparents, Theo."

"You weren't the only grandparent. Edward and Annabel did their share. She spent several summers with them either at the ranch or at Annabel's place in Colorado. How many times was she in Paris?"

"Twice."

"And how many years did she live with her parents?"

"All right, Theo. I see your point."

She sounded weary. He waited a moment.

"Perhaps I've only been using her as an excuse to go back to France. If I'm a bad influence, you see, I should go away, and I shouldn't leave Melrose in my house."

A late afternoon breeze riffled the surface of the fountain's pool. Rose, angry at Theo and herself, watched the distortions of her reflection in the water. How little I understand myself. Sixty-four next month and I'm as ignorant as I was at day one.

Theo reached for her hand. "That might be a part of your decision. It's not all. You seem to be in the humor to blame yourself for a good deal."

She began smiling, "Once you get started, Theo, it's hard to stop."

"I want you to stop. Try. Remember Melrose is a separate person."

"All right. I have only one son, and I saw his daughter as an extension of myself. I suppose it's egocentric. I'm sure Phillip would think it is incestuous." She threw both arms up in mock despair.

"You'll let her stay here then?"

"On two conditions. She has to call her parents once a week, and she must spread drop cloths if she paints."

"Good." He started up the steps to the garage apartment which had been his since Melrose returned. Because Rose had been expecting George to live there, it was furnished with a good bed, a club chair, and a desk. There was a small guest bedroom in the house. He preferred staying in the apartment where he wouldn't have to share a bathroom with anyone. He might have managed with one, but a man, even an old man, would be a daily interruption in two women's routines. Beside, Theo finally admitted to himself, he didn't want Melrose to catch him tiptoeing through the hall to her grandmother's room, not that he actually did tiptoe. He walked. Lately he hadn't been to Rose's room at all. She wasn't interested in having him in as long as her granddaughter was living there. When Melrose had left to see her parents, he and Rose shared a blissful week heightened by his own feeling of joy in the forbidden, an adolescent reaction no doubt. He was so many years away from that period of time in his life he decided he might as well recapture some part of it. The feelings he'd had about sex then had probably never truly left him; they had just been frozen after Kate's death.

Now he missed Rose. His fingers so longed to touch her he found himself clutching them together so he would not surprise her by suddenly grasping an arm or stroking the back of her neck when he passed. Soon, he reminded himself, his deprivations would be over. They would be in a stateroom together.

Rose's method of packing was to heap a selection of clothes on top of her bed, then put half of them back in the closet. This time she was thankful she'd winnowed her wardrobe out before returning to the U.S. She still had too many clothes it seemed.

Fortunately she'd saved some of the heavier things. It would be cooler in Paris. She'd already warned Theo.

Packing, she believed, was one of the most tiresome of human activities. Since she seldom worried about what she wore daily, why did she have to become perfectly dressed when traveling? If she needed anything, she knew the stores in Paris, which was more than she could say about those in Austin where all the places she'd known before had either vanished or metamorphosed into harrowing warehouses full of racks in malls. She couldn't quite understand how they were organized and wished for old department store signs that said "Sportswear" or "Better Dresses." In these vast new spaces she might wander alone half a day without meeting a clerk.

Anne Tomlin, who had driven her to her first encounter with a mall, objected, "Rose, Paris has huge stores, the *Galeries Lafayette, Samaritane*—"

"Yes, of course. I'm used to them though. Once you know where to look for whatever you need, big stores get smaller."

"All you have to do is get to know these."

"Yes, I suppose so," said Rose. But she hadn't bought anything. Now she was pleased she hadn't. Turning from her closet, she found Theo waiting in her doorway in the last rays of the late afternoon sun.

"I just realized I don't have a raincoat," he said. "I haven't needed one in so long. I think I lost it before moving over here."

"Let's both buy one in London. Then I won't have to pack mine now."

Theo stared down at the collection of clothes on her bed. "Rose." He lifted his head, "Wouldn't you like to come out. . . ? Wouldn't you like to stay in the apartment with me tonight?"

"You want me to sneak out of my own house?" At once Rose remembered late-dating when she was sixteen, moving slowly through the darkened kitchen so she could go out the back door to meet another boy after the first date brought her in the front. Her mother had been waiting for her in a blaze of light when she came home. Though a severe lecture on her lack of proper moral graces followed, her mother's words fell in a muddle on the shiny kitchen linoleum. All Rose cared about was not letting the first boy know she actually preferred the second. To her the moral question was how to avoid hurting feelings.

"Do you think Melrose will be waiting for you in the kitchen?" Theo asked.

"No. I worry that she'll know about us, and I don't want her to . . . not just yet. Don't be insulted, Theo. I realize how silly I sound."

Theo, seeing that they had switched roles, shook his head and began laughing.

Though she'd been invited Melrose did not go with them to New York. Instead she remained at Rose's.

"It's not time for her to go out wandering again," Theo said and added, "She's lucky she's got her grandmother's house for refuge."

Mr. Cantu had been hired as a caretaker; he was to come every week, and Ricardo would come with him to help.

Their leave-taking was everything Theo expected it to be; confetti falling, streamers flowing, champagne corks popping, horns tooting, messages from both his sons, flowers for Rose from Phillip and Melrose. When the clamor had quieted he stood by the rail glad for silence. As the ship slid past the Statue of Liberty, Rose asked him if he was worried about leaving.

"I could be," he acknowledged. "I could worry about being alive tomorrow, but I'm not." He smiled at her. "It doesn't matter if I die abroad. Any place will do for dying."

She put her hand over his while they leaned against the rail gazing out at the vast sea before them. He was venturing at last, not on his own terms quite; no doubt that was included in venturing.

ABOUT THE AUTHOR

Carolyn **Osborn** graduated from the University of Texas at Austin with a B.J. degree in 1955, and an M.A. in 1959. She has won awards from P.E.N., the Texas Institute of Letters, and a Distinguished Prose Award from *The Antioch Review* (2003). Her stories have been included in *The O. Henry Awards* (Doubleday, 1991) and *Lone Star Literature* (Norton, 2003), among numerous other anthologies. She is the author of several collections of short stories, including: *A Horse of Another Color* (University of Illinois Press, 1977), *The Fields of Memory* (Shearer Publishing, 1984), and *Warriors & Maidens* (Texas Christian University Press, 1991). The Book Club of Texas published an illustrated, specially bound edition of her story, *The Grands* (1990). In 2009, she received the Lon Tinkle Award from the Texas Institute of Letters.

ACKNOWLEDGMENTS

I am most grateful to Emily Fourmy Cutrer for her excellent biography, *The Art of the Woman: The Life and Work of Elizabet Ney* (1988), to Peter Flagg Maxson, architectural historian, who loaned me *Austin's Hyde Park...the first fifty years: 1891-1941* by Sarah and Thad Sitton, and to the unknown woman who told me the incident about the young boy's first vist to the Ney thereby providing the beginning of this book.

To my friends Angela Boone, Catherine Rogowski Pascale, Bonnie Swem Nelson and Mary Bess Whidden, my thanks for many years of encouragement. And my continual gratitude to my husband Joe Osborn, who is my own "best friend."

Thanks also to *The Texas Quarterly* and *The Antioch Review*, in which some stories excerpted from *Contrary People* first appeared.

Wings Press was founded in 1975 by Joanie Whitebird and Joseph Lomax, both deceased, as "an informal association of artists and cultural mythologists dedicated to the preservation of the literature of the nation of Texas." Publisher, editor and designer since 1995, Bryce Milligan is honored to carry on and expand that mission to include the finest in American writing—meaning all of the Americas—without commercial considerations clouding the choice to publish or not to publish.

Wings Press publishes multicultural books, chapbooks, ebooks, CDs and DVDs that, we hope, enlighten the human spirit and enliven the mind. Every person ever associated with Wings has been or is a writer, and we know well that writing is a transformational art form capable of changing the world, primarily by allowing us to glimpse something of each other's souls. Good writing is innovative, insightful, and interesting. But most of all it is honest.

Likewise, Wings Press is committed to treating the planet itself as a partner. Thus the press uses as much recycled material as possible, from the paper on which the books are printed to the boxes in which they are shipped. All inks and papers used meet or exceed United States health and safety requirements.

As Robert Dana wrote in *Against the Grain,* "Small press publishing is personal publishing. In essence, it's a matter of personal vision, personal taste and courage, and personal friendships." Welcome to the Wings Press community of readers.

WINGS PRESS

Colophon

This first edition of *Contrary People,* by Carolyn Osborn, has been printed on 55 pound Edwards Brothers Natural Paper containing a high percentage of recycled fiber. Titles have been set in Herculaneum type, the text in Adobe Caslon type. All Wings Press books are designed and produced by Bryce Milligan.

On-line catalogue and ordering
available at
www.wingspress.com

Wings Press titles are distributed
to the trade by the
Independent Publishers Group
www.ipgbook.com

Also available as an ebook.